PRAISE FOR GARRETT LEIGH

"Emotional and brilliant..."

— All About Romance

"Tastefully erotic ... more smart than smutty..."

— Publishers Weekly

"Powerful and compelling..."

— Foreword Reviews

FALLING FOR MY ROOMMATE

GARRETT LEIGH

Cover Art: Garrett Leigh @ Black Jazz Design

Editing: Posy Roberts @ Boho Edits

Proofing: Con Riley, Annabelle Jacobs, Alex Korent, Jennifer Meadows.

1

Sam

It didn't matter how many times I explained to my Yorkshire kin that the London pub I worked in was as civilised as you could get, they still thought I worked in a spit-and-sawdust boozer in Hackney, fighting knife crime and dodging bullets. The *Daily Mail* had a lot to answer for in the seaside town I called home.

Not that I called Whitby home anymore. I'd been a Londoner for eight years and couldn't see that changing. I loved city life. Even on weekdays, surrounded by yuppies and bankers with their bluster and excess.

I preferred Saturdays, though. The Fox was down the road from the Barbican and got enough custom from tourists and locals to keep things interesting. Lucky for me, today was Saturday, and it was getting late. Food service was over, leaving the tourists sipping cocktails and the locals chugging pints. The only exception was my flatmate in the corner, nursing his customary Diet Coke with ice and lemon and thumbing through his phone.

Micah caught my eye as I wove through the crowd collecting empty glasses. As ever, his dark gaze made me weak at the knees, but

I dampened the sensation down like a pro. I was happy with my place in his friend zone.

I had to be. There was nothing else . . . right?

Micah

The pub was busy, but Sam still breezed past every ten minutes to check on me, even though he knew I'd never finish the drink he'd put in front of me at six o'clock. Sometimes I wondered how on earth he hadn't figured out that I didn't frequent this shithole pub every weekend for the quality of its carbonated brown water. Most nights, though, I thanked my lucky stars that he liked me enough to let me stalk him at work all night long.

The thought made me smile as I glanced up at just the right time to catch his attention. His blue eyes sparkled at me across the crowded bar, and for a fleeting moment, stars aligned. Then some fucker called his name and he was gone, leaving me to curse the fact that his easy grin wasn't only for me.

I shook my head with my gaze still fixed on him. The bar was moodily dark, but somehow Sam's golden hair still glinted like the sun. He was wearing skinny jeans and Docs, a Motörhead T-shirt, and an apron that made his slim waist look tiny. He slipped between tables and stools, stacking glasses and wielding a wet cloth. Men and women alike were watching him like I was. And he had no idea. Because that was the thing about Sam: he was the most gorgeous bloke on the planet, and he had no fucking clue.

Still shaking my head, I went back to scrolling mindlessly through my phone. A few messages pinged in. I ignored most of them, but there was one I couldn't—Freddie Santos, an old teammate I accidentally owed my life to.

Freddie: *yo yo yo, where u at man?*

Micah: *same place I usually am, bro*

Freddie: *not that crap hole by Moorgate?*

Micah: *like you've ever taken the tube in your life*

Micah: *but yeah, that's where I'm at*

Freddie went quiet, and I hoped that was it. He was a genuine friend, but not one I liked enough to talk to more than once in a blue moon.

I returned to the tabloid news site I'd been perusing for no other reason than I was a bored masochist. Enough time had passed since my career-ending meltdown that I was no longer a regular in the red tops, but my mate Dom wasn't so lucky. He'd stepped away from the circus of elite football *years* ago, and yet somehow papped pics of him and his boyfriend still lit up my screen.

Mauling my bottom lip, I tapped through the images of my one-time teammate strolling through Regent's Park, hand-in-hand with his beautiful boyfriend. Resentment warred with admiration. Dom had been the first of us yanked out of the closet. To have his life flayed open for all to see, irrevocably blighting the career he'd spent his entire existence building. He'd walked away without looking back.

Me? Fuck. I'd clung on until it had nearly killed me, but that was a story for another day. The scar on my leg throbbed. I rubbed it through my jeans as a soft thumb appeared from nowhere and rescued my lip from my teeth.

"Stop brooding."

I treated Sam to a scowl we both knew I didn't mean. Not with him. Never with him. "I'm not brooding, I'm reading."

"Dude, the only shit you ever read are those wanky tabloids, and they always put you in a foul mood."

"I'm not in a foul mood."

"Oh no? So why are you glaring death craters into your phone screen?"

He had me there. But as luck would have it, Freddie saved the day.

Freddie: *i'm gonna swing by*

I held the message up for Sam to read as evidence of why I was giving my phone the stink eye. On cue, his lovely face folded into his own glower. "What does that knobhead want?"

"A drink, maybe? This *is* a pub."

"I meant in general. He only hits you up when he wants something."

"That's not true."

"Yes, it is."

"Be nice."

Sam huffed and stomped off, slender hips swinging. My hands balled into fists and I forced myself to avert my gaze and mentally prepare for the whirlwind that was Freddie Santos.

Ten minutes later, he breezed into the bar looking every inch the flash git that made footballers so popular and yet unpopular at the same time. Designer everything, *Peaky Blinders* hair-don't and a shit-eating grin that made even me, a by-product of his world, want to punch him in the face.

He dropped onto the bar stool next to me. "Duuuude, how's tricks?"

"Same as ever." I pocketed my phone, suppressing a sigh. "What brings you down these parts?"

"Looking for my wingman, aren't I?"

"I've never been your wingman."

"Course you have. What about those clubs in Rio? You were always by my side then."

"Not on purpose. There was nowhere else to stand."

Freddie rolled his eyes, but I was saved from further bullshit by Sam's sullen appearance behind the bar.

He fixed Freddie with a bland stare. "What can I get you?"

Freddie scanned the shelves behind Sam. "Suppose it's too much to ask for your champagne list?"

"Nope, but it'd be a short read, even for you."

Too dense to realise Sam was already cutting him down, Freddie let out a theatrical sigh. "Whatever. I'll have a vodka. Neat. And make it the good stuff; Micah's paying."

Sam turned away to fix the drink.

I thumped Freddie's arm as hard as I dared, considering the insurance policies his club probably had on his body. "Why am I paying?

You know I take home a couple of grand a month now. That's a *month*, dude. Not an hour."

Freddie shrugged, rubbing his arm. "I was joking. Trying to get a rise out of your pretty roommate. You know he gets territorial over you."

"I think it's more he's pegged you for a prize wanker."

I'd never spoken truer words, but they didn't sound the same in my flat London accent. Sam's warm, northern brogue made everything magic. I heard it in my dreams, awake, asleep, always.

Freddie nudged me. "I don't care what your dude thinks of me, man."

"He's not my dude."

"Uh-huh. Anyway, I really did come by to drag you out. A bunch of us are heading to that new joint by the river tonight, the one with the burlesque show and the titty bar. Come with me?"

I stared at him like he'd grown horns. Like he hadn't been the one to hold my hand when the London Transport Police had scraped me off the Tube tracks. "Are you kidding me? Why the fuck would I want to go to a titty bar?"

"Dunno. Maybe to spend some time with your mates? People who haven't seen you for months and months and months?"

There was a damn good reason for that: those arseholes hadn't ever been my fucking friends. But I knew Freddie, and it was loaded conversations like this that kept me from icing him out of my life. As clumsy and offensive as he was, he really did care.

A shot of vodka appeared on the bar. I didn't dare look up, but I felt Sam's presence like a second skin.

Freddie didn't spare Sam a glance either. He prodded me in the ribs. "So? What are you saying? You wanna come out?"

"I'm not saying anything remotely like that. Even without the titty bar, it's not my scene. Not anymore."

The conversation went round in circles, but eventually, Freddie necked his vodka, dropped a fifty on the bar—*show off*—and left. By then, the bar had quieted. On instinct, I searched out Sam. He was by the fire exit, sweeping the battered wooden floor. My gaze zeroed in on his long, lean legs encased in gunmetal denim, his elegant hands, and finally his dazzling grin.

He ambled over to me. "Dickhead gone home?"

"As if. He's off out. Wanted me to go with him."

"Didn't fancy it?"

"What do you think?"

"That your mate is a bit of a twat, but you should probably get out more."

"To a strip club by the river?"

Sam grimaced. "Okay. Maybe not. I stand by the twat comment, though."

"He left you a forty-quid tip."

"He's still a prick."

Frustration, laced with a heavy dose of guilt washed over me. "He can't help acting up. When you're young and surrounded by that lunacy, it's hard to know any better."

"He's not that young."

"Not by playing standards, maybe, but in real life he is. Why can't you trust me when I say he's a nice bloke underneath it all?"

Sam shrugged. "Because you've never told me why. You let him prance around in front of me like a peacock and expect me to just believe you that he's something else entirely."

"You think I'd lie to you?"

"No, I think you're too nice for your own good."

I laughed. Couldn't help it. In the last six months, Sam had got to know me better than anyone else had in years, but fuck, he still had so much to learn. "I'm not nice."

"You are. But don't worry, I'll never tell anyone."

2

Sam

Micah sent me a soft grin across the breakfast bar and accepted the plate of bagels, smoked salmon, and soft scrambled eggs. "Thanks. You didn't have to do that."

He had no idea how untrue that statement was. When he'd first answered my ad for a flat-share and moved in, he'd spent days and days alone in his room. The only way I'd coaxed him out was with food, and six months into our roomie-hood, it was a habit I'd yet to break. "I was up anyway."

Lies. All lies. But who the fuck cared if I'd jumped out of bed the moment I'd heard Micah limping out of his bedroom?

Not me.

I fixed my own plate and rounded the breakfast bar to claim my seat beside him. He was scrolling through his phone again. I nudged him. "You're on that thing so much I'm starting to think you've got a Grindr account."

Micah snorted. "A new Grindr account, you mean. You know what happened with the last one."

Of course I did. Even without the left leg that dragged behind him when he walked, the whole world knew that a casual hook-up had sold him out to the tabloids, and the threat of exposure had driven him to an "incident" on the London Underground. I'd never understand why a career spent kicking a leather ball around a field was so important, but then working in the bar was the most exciting thing I'd ever done, so what did I know?

I found a smile from somewhere and pasted it onto my face. "Just because it didn't pan out the first time doesn't mean you're doomed to a lifetime of gay bachelorhood. Whether you want to be or not, you're out now—"

"I do want to be."

"—so you might as well hook up. There must be a thousand blokes out there who'd want to be with you."

Micah slid me a look I couldn't decipher. "I don't want a thousand blokes."

"Well, not all at once. That's beyond an orgy, eh?"

"If you say so. I've never had one."

So the papers had lied about that too. I made a note in my *Micah files* and, not for the first time, wished that I'd known absolutely nothing about him until he'd rocked up on my doorstep. It was so unfair. I had the privilege of privacy that he hadn't had since he'd signed his life away as a football-mad teenager. He knew of me what I wanted him to. *I* knew he was lucky to be walking at all. That he'd been sectioned for two weeks, and his entire family had disowned him. And he'd never told me a fucking thing.

I poured more coffee and changed the subject, wittering away about bullshit gossip from the bar until Micah ditched his phone and started to eat. As usual, a good feed cheered him up and brought him alive in ways that made dragging my tired self out of bed three hours before I wanted to totally worthwhile. The changes in him were subtle, but I saw them like beacons in the dark, lighting the way to his kind, funny, and clever soul. If only he knew how he made my heart skip. Actually, scratch that. I was glad he didn't. Our friendship meant the world to me. Spoiling it because I couldn't contain myself would be the worst thing that could ever happen.

To both of us.

After breakfast, he stretched and limped off to the bathroom. The shower turned on, and steam billowed out through the warped door he'd, as usual, neglected to close properly.

It took every ounce of restraint I possessed not to peek. I busied myself rinsing plates and stacking the dishwasher. Then I retreated to my room and crawled back into bed. I flicked the TV on and lost myself in an episode of *Columbo* until a light tap roused me.

Micah stood in the doorway, dressed in sweats and a hoodie, hair still damp but effortlessly cool next to my grungy bedhead. "Got a client. Be back around four. What shift are you working?"

"Four to twelve."

"Oh." His cautiously open expression closed off. "I thought it was five."

"It was, but someone needs to go home early from the lunch shift."

"Why's that your problem?"

"It's not. But an extra few quid isn't going to do me any harm. We haven't all got millions in the bank, you know."

"I haven't got millions in the bank either. I spent it all on horses, coke, and escorts when I was living my best straight life, but thanks for the reminder."

Gallows humour softened the punch of his words, but I felt the impact in my chest all the same. "Your best life is still out there. You just have to go somewhere other than the gym and the shithole I work at."

"I like the gym, and I like where you work."

I'd never quite understood why, on either count. The gym was the home of the devil, and Micah hated crowds and drinkers, so why he hung out at the Fox every weekend was a mystery to me. "You're a freak."

"Tell me something I don't know. Text me if you need anything, yeah?"

"I will."

He left and I followed his lead of taking a shower and getting ready for work. During the week, when Micah was home alone while I worked, I'd curse the fact that my job demanded such unsociable hours, but weekends were different, Saturdays and Sundays. I knew he'd come and see me.

Because he always did.

I glanced across the bar and stifled a laugh. Micah caught me and treated me to a rueful grin, but it was brief, his attention too in demand to be wasted on the likes of me.

Or, at least, that's what the tipsy lady in the high heels and floaty skirt probably thought. I wasn't her type. Too cute, according to her. And that was fine by me. As cougars went, she was sweet and nowhere near the worst the bar had to offer, but a woman's beautiful body did nothing for me. I was gay, gay, and throw in a little more gay.

I wasn't sure about Micah. Before his secret life of Grindr had been exposed to the world, he'd hit the gossip pages with a different girl every week—supermodels, pop stars, socialites. I knew he was bisexual, but I'd never got round to asking him how much of the rest of it was real, perhaps because I was scared of his answer.

A customer rapped his knuckles on the bar. I blinked, gaze flitting between him and Micah, who was now frowning at me as if I'd lost my mind. *Whoops. Staring again.* I snapped back into work mode and served the man his jug of ale and a pork pie. By the time I was done, Micah had escaped the clutches of the gin-soaked woman. He came to the bar. Two of my colleagues had clocked off for the night and were putting away a few sherbets before they went home. They eyed Micah as he settled in beside them but knew better than to try and engage him. Micah had no time for anyone who wasn't me or Freddie. Not anymore.

The girls at the bar were talking about boys. Before Micah, I might've joined in, but now I just listened, smirking in the appropriate places as I polished glasses and studied Micah's profile.

He was still in his gym clothes. His dark hair was dry now, and despite the chill in the air, he'd pushed his sleeves up, revealing the pocket-watch tattoo sleeves on his strong forearms. Micah had the best skin, smooth and light brown; I spent far too much time imagining how it would feel beneath my fingertips.

His glass was half-empty. I reached for it and jerked my head at the soda pumps. "Top-up?"

"Nah." He shook his head and shifted his weight around. "As much as I'm enjoying finding out about every borough man's junk, I'm gonna go home."

He murmured the words as if they were only for me, but the girls beside him heard all the same.

"Aw, come on, Micah." Céleste poked his arm. "You know you're having fun, really. Come get drunk with us. Sam does all the time."

"I know. I hear him falling up the stairs when he's trying to get into the flat."

"It's true," I admitted. "I can't remember the last time you didn't have to get up and let me in."

Micah smirked a little at that. True facts, you see. But I could tell he was done for the night. Despite further protests from the girls at the bar, he pulled his hood up and left.

We all watched him go. The girls for obvious reasons. Me because I was anxious the icy weather would make the pavements slippery for him. And the other reasons. Because it was impossible to look at Micah and not notice how beautiful he was.

Céleste sighed. "He's so dreamy."

"He's moody as fuck," Jennifer countered. "Who's got time for that?"

"Who needs to have time for it when it's never going to happen?" Céleste said. "He's gay, right? All the best ones are."

Their conversation moved on. The glass in my hand creaked, and I realised I was clutching it in a death grip. I set it down, half proud Céleste considered Micah amongst the best dudes in town, and half furious that they'd had the gall to discuss him in the first place. *He's not a piece of fucking meat.*

I left the bar and busied myself cleaning tables as the pub

emptied out. Irritation buzzed in my veins, but I couldn't quite put my finger on why. The girls hadn't said anything that wasn't true. Micah *was* moody, and he was also the nicest dude I'd ever known. Sweet, considerate, and fiercely protective of the handful of people on the planet he actually liked. One day, when he was ready, he'd make someone an amazing—

"Sam?"

"Hmm?" I spun around. Céleste was behind me, perfect brow raised. "Sorry, what?"

"You look like your dog just died."

"I don't have a dog."

"I wasn't being literal, sweetie. Just stating facts that your face is telling me the worst thing in the world just happened to you."

I made an effort to school my features. "Sorry. In a world of my own. Did you need me for something?"

Céleste took my arm and towed me away from the table I was working on and into the shadows of the faithful fire exit. "I wanted to apologise for bringing Micah into our gossip pool like that earlier. We didn't mean anything by it. I know you two are close."

"I didn't have a problem with it. It's none of my business."

"What isn't? The screechy conversations me and my girls have at a public bar, or Micah's love life?"

"Either."

"Uh-huh." Céleste sent me a smirk that called bullshit. "So that's why you get so pissy anytime someone mentions how hot he is?"

"I don't get pissy."

"Liar. Look, I can't control what other people say, but if it helps, I can stop the girls drooling over him in front of you."

"Why the fuck—" Dammit. What the hell was I supposed to say? Denying that I hated it when Céleste—no, *anyone*—talked about Micah that way was pointless, but trying to control a narrative that didn't belong to me was even worse. "Don't do anything on my account, okay? Me and Micah are just friends. Flatmates. Who fancies him has got nothing to do with me."

"So you wouldn't mind if I set him up with my cousin then?"

"What?"

"My cousin. He's coming over from Paris next month, and I think him and Micah would get on great."

"How the hell would you think that when you don't know Micah?"

Céleste gave me a long look.

I stared her down for all of three seconds before waving my hands in frustration. "Whatever. Do what you want. I'm not his fucking mother."

Céleste kissed her teeth and left me in peace to rage sweep the floor, my anger both at her for bringing such a stupid conversation to me and myself for acting as if I had any claim on Micah. I didn't get to choose if he hooked up with Céleste's cousin. *He* did. And because I'd been an arse about it, he'd probably never get the chance.

Which is totally unfair. You know he hasn't got any queer friends.

It was true. Not real ones, anyway. Not people he could talk to, lean on, and meet other queer people through. New people. Who weren't me.

So you're not queer and/or his friend?

Of course I was. On both counts. I was Captain-fucking-Queer. If anyone could help Micah expand his sexually social horizons, it was me. Which meant I'd been a dick to Céleste *and* to him in one fell swoop.

Super.

At some point, I'd have to dissect my soul and figure out why once and for all. But it was late, and I was tired. All I wanted was a cold walk home to one of Micah's signature mugs of cinnamon cocoa and a platonic hug before bed.

Micah

I hated coming back to the flat when Sam wasn't there. When he was, it felt like home. When he wasn't, it was empty rooms and the noise in my head.

It helped that he was a messy mofo. Clearing up after him saved me hours of pacing our small space, and . . . I liked doing it. After all the hot dinners he'd put in my belly, picking up his cute socks was the least I could do.

And they were fucking cute. Pirates this time. It had been ladybirds yesterday, French bulldog puppies the day before. I loaded a wash into the machine and set the time delay for it to start the next morning. Then I kicked around, tidying shit that was already tidy while I watched the clock, counting the minutes until Sam was due home. Some nights he stayed to get drunk with his girls after hours, but he hadn't seemed in the mood tonight. Every time I'd looked up, he'd been staring into space, which meant he had the hump or he was hungry.

With that in mind, I drifted to the fridge and opened it. Sam had done the shopping and filled the shelves with things I liked, even though I'd never told him what I liked. I wished I knew what he liked. Some days I stood in the shop, staring at the shelves and imagining I was a different man. A better man. The kind of man who could load up the basket and come home and cook a meal for the boy who'd made his life bearable again. But I wasn't that man. Never had been. And a scar that stretched from the back of my thigh to the middle of my shin would never change that.

What are you bitching about your leg for? Don't you ever get bored of that shit?

The front door opened. Sam shuffled through it, blond hair dishevelled, eyes hooded and tired. He wrenched his key from the lock and kicked the door shut. It banged. He winced, and I wanted to tell him not to care about our dickhead neighbours, but there was no point. He cared. I didn't. End of.

I closed the fridge. Had second thoughts and opened it again.

Sam chuckled from the hallway and joined me in the kitchen. "Are you doing that thing again where you expect the fridge to make you a toasted sandwich?"

"Maybe. You don't think it's unreasonable that fridges don't do that in an age where we can control the heating from our phones?"

"It's totally unreasonable, but it's not changing anytime soon, unless you have a design patent I don't know about." Sam reached around me and grabbed ham, cheese, and mustard from the top shelf. "Sit."

"No. You're the one who's been on his feet all night. I'll do it."

For a moment he looked as though he might argue—he usually did—then he sighed and stepped away. "Whatevs. Go heavy on the mustard, yeah? My synapses need singeing."

"Do you mean sinuses?"

"Nope."

He disappeared. A minute later, the shower turned on, and I got to work lugging his Panini press out of the cupboard. I slathered hot English mustard on seeded bread and layered on smoked ham and cheddar cheese. Before Sam, I'd forgotten the simple joy of a toastie —I'd forgotten a lot of things—but seeing as they were amongst the only things I could cook, and he *loved* them, I made them all the time.

I toasted four sandwiches and chucked them on the one big plate we owned: the one with Father Christmas painted onto it. Loaded up with mango juice—Sam's other favourite thing—I limped back to the living room and dropped my wares on the coffee table. No longer keyed up and waiting for Sam, energy drained from me. The couch called my name. I sank onto it, perversely enjoying its lumps and bumps, the rough material, and the slight scent of damp from where it had languished in Sam's parents' garage for ten years before he'd brought it here. In my old place, in my old damn-fucking *life*, I'd had an eight-seater monstrosity that had barely filled the corner of my swanky living room. Sometimes, I heard the creak of the leather in my dreams and woke up sweating.

Sam emerged from the bathroom, a pair of sweats hanging from his slender hips, towelling his hair dry, and . . . shirtless.

Averting my gaze, I nodded at the plate of sandwiches. "Eat up."

"You didn't start without me?"

"As if I would, though I should've. Eating with you is like having twelve siblings."

Sam sniggered, but it was muffled by the ginormous bite of food he'd crammed in his mouth.

Cute as fuck.

I claimed a sandwich and made short work of it while Sam polished off the other three. He was quiet, which wasn't unusual after a long shift, and I was hardly Mr Chatty, but for some reason, tonight his silence got under my skin. I nudged him. "Everything okay?"

"Hmm?"

"You're quiet. Have I upset you?"

Sam's bemusement deepened. "Why do you always assume you've upset me? You've literally never upset me in your life."

That made him unique. Of everyone I'd ever been close to, I couldn't pinpoint any who'd make that statement so confidently. "Sorry. I just . . ."

"What?" Sam leaned closer. His thigh brushed my hip, then closed the distance between us so his leg was flush against mine. "Have *I* upset *you*?"

"What? No! Why would you say that?"

"Because I thought that's what we were doing—asking ridiculous questions." He scanned the coffee table, clearly seeking more food. His gaze fell on the book he'd brought back from the library for me a few days ago. "Did you start this yet?"

"Um . . . yeah."

"Are you lying?"

"No."

Sam picked the book up—*City of Thieves*—and traced the title with his finger. "Tell me something about it."

"They all die at the end?"

He pouted. "When I said it was written by one of the *Game of*

Thrones dudes, I didn't mean it was the same. You haven't even picked it up, have you?"

"Course I have."

"Then tell me something about it."

"They're going to kill the chicken."

"Huh?"

I took the book from him and flipped it to the page where I'd abandoned it. "They just found the dude with the chicken. They're going to take it off him and kill it, so I'm out. I don't want to read that shit."

Sam pursed his lips, a telltale sign he was trying not to laugh. "You're really going to read that much of a book, then discard it because some young boys in a starving city are going to eat a pet chicken? Well, cockerel, actually, but the point still applies."

"I don't care what the point is. I don't like it."

Sam's expression softened. He took the book from me and returned it to the coffee table. "I forget how sweet you are."

I scowled. "Fuck off."

"I will not. It's true."

"It's really not. You're the only person in the entire world who has ever used that word to describe me."

"Then maybe the world needs to know you better."

"I'd rather it didn't."

Sam sighed again and flopped back on the couch. "I know you think the world has seen enough of you to last just about forever, but that doesn't mean you should hide away for the rest of your life."

"I'm not hiding."

"No? When was the last time you went anywhere that wasn't my place of work or yours?"

"Yesterday. I went to the hospital for a 'wellbeing check' on my mental health."

"I meant somewhere you wanted to go."

"I did want to go there. It's good for me to know I'm doing okay."

Sam closed his eyes. "Don't be so fucking awkward. I mean fun stuff, Micah. Like, social stuff. Even going out with Freddie Fuckwit has got to be better than watching me pull pints every night."

I didn't watch Sam work *every* night, but I got the feeling that arguing with him right now would get me nowhere, even though I wanted with all my heart for him to shut the fuck up. "You want me to go out with Freddie? Cos he asked me the other night."

"Why didn't you go?"

"Because I'm a washed-up queer with a bum leg and zero interest in caning it in some fuckhead titty club. I'd rather go to the library with you."

"Really?" Sam's left eye slid open. "Because I'll totally make you go."

"When?"

"Tomorrow. I need to get some stuff for my course."

"Fine by me."

"Don't joke about the library, Micah. It's my church."

"I'm not joking."

Sam cracked both his eyes and sat up. "Are you serious? You're going to loaf it into town with me to the library and pick your own damn books for a change?"

"It's three minutes down the road, fam. And don't be acting like I've never gone there with you before."

"Like, once. Six months ago, when you first moved in, and only because you didn't want to get caught in the rain."

Sometimes I forgot it had been less than a year since my agent had done one last thing for me before we'd parted ways and found me a discreet and affordable flat-share. In reality, I could've bought Sam's grandparents' place twice over with the money I had left from the glory days—*insert sarcasm*—but renting his spare room had saved me from something I couldn't describe. I'd go to the library with him every day for the rest of my life if he wanted me to. I owed him far more than that.

3

Sam

Micah liked the library. He might not have known it yet, but I did. And it made perfect sense. The library building was big enough to get lost in, but cosy enough that he could hide in the corner if he wanted to and no one would notice him. Not that anyone was lurking around the library expecting to see premiership football players checking out the crime fiction.

I left him with a stack of gangster novels and retreated to the English lit section. I found the annotated copy of *The Kite Runner* I needed and dumped it on a nearby table. *Tell me again why you thought going back to school to get your English A-level was a good idea?*

Because I didn't want to work in a fucking bar all my life. Or, at least, I hadn't before I'd started. Now a future of pulling pints and mixing hipster G&Ts was looking decidedly favourable compared to the part-time course that was driving me up the wall.

I made notes for a full half hour before Micah came to find me. He was empty-handed. "Didn't find anything you liked?"

"Nope. What are you reading?"

"*The Kite Runner*. It's for my course."

Micah flopped into the seat beside me and slid the book towards him. “Is it old?”

“Not really. It was published in 2003.”

“Huh. I thought you’d be doing Shakespeare or some shit.”

“Nope. This one, *Frankenstein*, and *A Streetcar Named Desire*.”

Micah looked suitably unimpressed, but that was his general expression for everything. After I’d met him and agreed to rent him my spare room, I’d looked him up on YouTube. Watched football videos and read tabloid articles about him. The gossip sites were the worst—the wild-eyed photos and sleazy poses with faceless women. In Micah the football player, I saw a man living his dream, even if that dream was something he no longer believed in. The man in the tabloid photos was an empty soul I didn’t recognise.

“What’s it about?” Micah asked.

“Two boys living in Afghanistan. At least that’s how it starts. They’re childhood friends who fly kites together. One is the son of a wealthy man, the other the son of the wealthy man’s servant.”

“What are the . . . fuck, I’ve forgotten what they’re called. The things you write on that whiteboard?”

“Themes?”

“Yeah, that’s it. Themes.”

“Guilt and redemption, mostly.

“Redemption?”

“Uh-huh. You wanna read it?”

“Nope. I’ll watch the film with you if you can promise me you’ll stay awake till the end.”

The prospect of spending an extended amount of time huddled on my shitty couch with him was enough to keep me awake for a week. “If I promise you that, will you go and pick an actual book off the shelf and take it home?”

“Are you going to sit me at the kitchen table and make me read it?”

“If we had a kitchen table, yes.”

“Why are you so obsessed with me reading books?”

“I’m not obsessed with anything.” *Except you.* And the truth was, I wanted Micah to read so he had the privilege I'd been gifted the moment I'd picked up my first Judy Blume book, the gift of leaving my life behind to live that of a thousand others. Not that my life had been particularly bad, but Micah's had, and he deserved respite from his own head. From whatever made his eyes dark and his pillowy lips pull down. "I'll watch the film with you."

Micah nodded. "Deal, and as payment for me picking out a different book, you can come to the gym with me in the morning."

Fuck. My. Life.

Micah

I honestly had zero intention of dragging Sam from his warm bed on a cold February morning and hustling him down the gym. It was just that banter with him was so fucking healing, I let it get out of hand.

Which was how I found myself lurking in his bedroom doorway at dawn the next day, watching him sleep. *You're such a creeper.*

Facts. But I couldn't make myself move, and, for once, my stiff leg wasn't to blame. My obsession with Sam was all in my heart, and no matter how hard I tried to get over it, the rush of feels I got every time he looked my way only seemed to grow.

Not that I understood it. I mean, Sam was amazing, so I got that, but what I didn't get was why he affected me so much. Until him, the bloke side of my sexuality had been all about sex, an itch that had to be scratched or I'd lose my fucking mind. Any real feelings—and they'd been pretty damn rare—had been for women, for the girlfriends I couldn't seem to keep for more than a hot minute. And even then, I'd never been drawn to *anyone* the way I was to Sam. He'd put a spell on me or some shit.

"Sexuality is complicated, you know that. Stop trying to put yourself in a box. Or at least build your own box, man."

Sam shifted in his sleep as the only sensible conversation I'd had with Dom since the accident echoed in my head. I wished I'd talked to him more, but at the time, it hadn't seemed fair to drop my troubles on him when he'd done so well at escaping his own.

"Micah?"

I blinked. Sam was awake and staring at me, though it was hard to tell if he was conscious enough to know which way was up. Sometimes it took him a while. "Sorry. Was gonna hustle you to the gym, but you looked too cute."

He rubbed his face. "I'm awake. I can come."

"Nah. Sleep. I'll bring you something from the bakery."

"Not that icky protein porridge."

"I know, I know. I'll make it good."

Laughing, I backed away from his door and fled the flat as fast as my limping would allow without making me look drunk. It was cold outside. I pulled my hood up to hide from the wind, but my brief encounter with Sam had warmed me from the inside out, so I didn't mind the bitter chill. I shuffled all the way to the gym with him filling my thoughts and almost forgot my own apprehension for the place until it appeared in front of me.

A year ago, exercise had been something I did without thinking. Like breathing. Up in Manchester, I'd rolled out of bed every day like the good little robot, went to training, played matches, and generally lived like an arsehole with no repercussions. It was like that for years. Then I'd switched clubs. Moved to London with zero clue of how different it would be from up north. How many eyes would be on me, and just how fast I'd unravel under the scrutiny.

And *fuck,* did I unravel.

But I didn't have the spoons to think about that today. If I wanted to be mobile for the next twenty-four hours, I had a workout to do before the world woke up and joined me.

"So, you don't come to the gym, and somehow I still have to go to a Valentine's party at the pub? Fuck off, mate."

Sam grinned from his bed, sugar from the lemon-raspberry

doughnut I'd brought him for breakfast all over his lovely face. I tracked his tongue as it darted out to lick his lips. Caught myself and tried to focus on his counterargument.

". . . you don't *have* to go anywhere," he said. "But there's going to be loads of single people there, men and women, so what harm could it do?"

"Single people? What the fuck has that got to do with anything?"

Sam shrugged, averted his gaze, and brushed crumbs from his bed. "Nothing, really. But don't you think you should get out a bit more? Meet new people?"

"New *single* people?"

"Or not. Whatever. Look, it's not a big deal. You'd probably have been there anyway."

"Says who?"

"Says custom and practice. You always come to the pub on Saturday nights."

Irritation, raw and irrational, ripped through me. I *did* go to the pub every Saturday, but not because I wanted to hang out with a bunch of drunk douches, and certainly not because I wanted to hook up with any of those clowns. How could he not know that? "Well, I'm not coming *this* Saturday. I've got plans."

"What plans?"

"Plans with Freddie."

A flash of something I couldn't decipher darkened Sam's features. "You're going out with Freddie?"

"Uh-huh."

"Where?"

"Dunno. Some club."

Sam opened his mouth. Shut it again. And it took every bit of remaining dickhead I had not to retract every fucking word. Every lie. But what did it matter? He only wanted me to come to the stupid Valentine's party so I could make new friends and stop emotionally leeching off him.

"Anyway." I pushed off his doorframe for the second time that day.

"I've got to get back to the gym for a client. I only came to give you your doughnut."

Sam wiped his face, expression a blank study. "Thanks. Have a good day."

As if. After that conversation, I was going to have the worst day ever.

4

Sam

"Why did you invite him to a singles night if you want to get in his pants yourself?"

I groaned, already regretting that I'd chosen Céleste to confess my woes to. "It's not even a singles night. I just mentioned that there'd be lots of singles here."

"Because of the cheap drinks we're offering specifically to single people. Face it, honey, it's a singles night."

"Yeah, but that's not what I said to him."

"Doesn't matter." Céleste dumped a bucket of sliced lemons on the bar. "That's what he heard, and *that's* what's pissed him off so much."

"He's not pissed off. He's, uh, busy."

"Too busy to babysit you like he does every weekend? Uh-uh, babes. That boy is as hung up on you as you are on him."

"He really isn't. He's annoyed with me for interfering in his life. Micah hates stuff like that and stuff like *this*." I gestured around the bar that was usually a traditional London boozer and was now decked out in scarlet sugar paper. "I don't blame him for picking Freddie instead."

"So what are you going to do?"

"Nothing?"

Céleste's hard stare told me that was the wrong answer. I thought again but came up none the wiser. She was wrong about Micah having feelings for me beyond friendship—he was so closed off to the world I was lucky he gave me the time of day in the first place—but perhaps she was right that I needed to do something to fix the weird stalemate between us. Micah could be moody, quiet, and withdrawn, but it had been three days since he'd stayed up late enough to say goodnight, and his bedroom door had remained shut every morning.

I miss him.

I left Céleste restocking the mixers and skulked outside under the pretence of emptying the bins, a job I detested more than the gym. Hiding in the shadows, I fished my phone from my apron and opened WhatsApp. My message thread with Micah was brief. He wasn't much of a communicator beyond asking me to get some milk on the way home or sending me random memes, and I often found he hadn't been online since our last conversation days ago, but he'd been active all day . . . not that I'd looked or anything.

He's going out tonight, remember? With Freddie.

Of course he was. I swallowed my distaste and tried to figure a banal way to get him to talk to me. Sad as it was, I needed to check in with him. To know he was okay, *and* to soothe my own anxieties. Weird vibes with Micah were bad for my mental health and clear evidence, if I even needed it, that messing with our friendship was a bad idea.

Sam: . . . *did you eat dinner?*

Smooth. Real smooth. I waited a moment to see if he'd come online to read it, but the ticks beside it stayed resolutely grey.

Damn it. Maybe he wouldn't respond. Maybe it would be the first message I ever sent that he ignored. Regardless, I didn't have time to wait and find out.

I trudged back inside. Céleste sent me a sympathetic smile—*how does she know?*—but I blanked her and threw myself into serving the weekend crowd that was growing by the second. The district might've been a dead zone, but the Fox knew how to smash a Saturday, and for once I was glad of the rising tide. It carried me until I came up for air a few hours later, and by then, Micah had responded.

In the bathroom, I held my breath as I opened the message.

Micah: *yes. did u?*

Three words, but I'd take them. I tapped out a reply.

Sam: *no, too busy. might get a cheeky kebab later*

Micah read the message. And then . . . nothing. He stayed online but didn't reply.

I squeezed my phone in a death grip. My brain filled with images of him partying in some bullshit club with Freddie, throwing drinks back, snorting coke, surrounded by leeches. And him liking it. It was a thousand moons away from the Micah I knew, but not the Micah that Freddie knew. That was their world. Micah had stepped away from it for a long time, but he'd never said he wouldn't go back. Until now, I'd never considered that he wanted to. But what the hell did I know? And what right did I have to an opinion on it?

Once more for the back, I was Micah's roommate, not his mother.

I abandoned the toilet and went back to work. Another hour passed, and as the knot in my chest grew, so did the snarl in my belly that reminded me I hadn't eaten all day.

It was a rare phenomenon that I didn't get around to stuffing my face with something. And hunger—when I had no chance of rectifying it any time soon—always put me in a bad mood. Add-in some heavy Micah blues, and I was about ready to deck the next idiot who thought it was okay to tug on my apron strings.

"You look like you're about to chin someone."

"I am," I answered without thinking before the gravelly voice, not raised in the slightest despite the boom of the crowd, hit home.

Micah. I spun around, half-convinced I'd imagined him, but there he was, leaning on the bar, a foil-wrapped parcel clutched in his hand. "What are you doing here?"

He shrugged. "I know how you get when you skip meals, so I brought you something to eat."

I worked in a pub with a fully serviced bar menu. All around me, orders of chips, retro whitebait, and hipster halloumi fries were being served on slate-grey tiles. There were any number of things I could've eaten if I'd had the inclination, but nothing would've come close to the foil-wrapped treasure Micah had brought me from home. "You brought me a toastie?"

"Yeah."

"Ham and cheese?"

"Yeah."

"Mustard?"

"Of course. Do you think I don't know you?"

And there was the problem. He *did* know me, probably better than anyone else ever had, but there was one vital piece of information he'd never learned and he never could: that I was completely and irrevocably in love with him.

Nice Twilight reference, you sad fuck.

But still. It was true.

I took the sandwich and signalled to Céleste that I was taking a long-overdue break. She swept her gaze over Micah while he wasn't looking and gave me a knowing smirk, but I turned my back on her and tugged Micah into the alcove reserved for staff.

He found yet something else to lean against. "It's crazy busy in here tonight."

"All-night happy hour." I unwrapped my still-warm toasted sandwich and took a bite. Like magic, the promise of mustard-hot food hitting my stomach soothed my soul. A little bit, anyway. I still had an unrequited crush on my roommate. "You wanna drink?"

"Nah. I've got to get an Uber to Knightsbridge."

Somehow I'd made myself forget about his big night out. My chewing slowed as I eyed his choice of outfit—dark jeans, boots, and a sweatshirt that had, once upon a time, probably cost more than my entire wardrobe. "That's what you're wearing?"

Micah fiddled with his cuffs. "What's wrong with it?"

"Nothing. I'm just in awe that you can hit London's swankiest clubs in jeans and a jumper."

"Yeah, well. They're the only clothes I own that aren't made for the gym. I left everything else at my old flat."

I already knew that. Micah had moved into my nan's old place with a suitcase, a cardboard box, and very little trace of the life he'd led as a top-flight footballer. Without the lurid tabloid articles documenting his tragic fall from grace, I'd have had no idea who he was. "You look nice."

"Thanks. I don't want to go."

So don't go. Stay here with me. "You'll be all right once you get there."

"If you say so. Listen, uh, we never got round to watching that film. You wanna tomorrow?"

"I'm working at twelve."

"I know. I figured maybe we could have a Sunday morning on the couch with those omelettes you like?"

"You mean the omelettes *I make* that *you* like?"

"Yeah, those ones. I'm training a client at seven, then I'm gonna swim, but I'll be home by nine."

The prospect of getting up so early on a Sunday morning after a manic Saturday night on the bar made me feel slightly ill, but the promise of a few hours on the couch with Micah was too enchanting to pass up. I swallowed the last of my sandwich. "Deal. Text me when you're on your way and I'll get the coffee on."

"I won't see you tonight?"

"Depends what time you get home."

I couldn't keep the sour note out of my voice, but if Micah noticed, it didn't show. He nodded and backed up. "I'll see you when I see you then."

"Hey."

He stopped. "What?"

I stood and opened my arms.

He stepped into them without blinking and wrapped his own around me, embracing me in the platonic hug we'd cultivated since the first time I'd come home drunk after he'd moved in. I'd insisted on hugging him that night and had just about died from embarrassment the next morning, but somehow, when we were speaking to each other, at least, it had become a tradition. Not too long or too tight, they were always perfect, like now, as Micah stepped away with a soft smile that hadn't been there before. He squeezed my shoulders. "Have a good night."

I smiled back. "You too."

Micah

I felt like a kid on Christmas Eve, wishing the night away so I could get to the morning already. The last few days had been weird. It wasn't often that me and Sam didn't vibe well, and I'd barely slept before he'd hugged me happy again in the dingy corner of that godforsaken pub.

The pub I'd have given my good leg to be stood in right now rather than the banal celeb haunt Freddie had dragged me to. I didn't drink much these days, especially in public, so I waved away the top price champagne and stuck to Diet Coke. By ten o'clock I had a carbonated bubble in my stomach and a headache. I wanted to go home, but I couldn't face the empty flat . . . or being alone with my imagination. A sober night out with Freddie was as ridiculous as I'd feared it would be, but it was better than picturing Sam surrounded by the throngs of hot singles I'd seen in the Fox. Or considering the possibility that he'd wanted me to hook up there because that's what he was planning on doing too.

Not that the two things were connected in any way that didn't exist inside my head.

A girl shimmied up to me, dressed in a tight glittery dress that made her look like an angel. She had long, dark hair and full lips, surgically enhanced breasts, and flawless skin. The old me would've been on that like white on rice, but I cringed as she wrapped herself around me.

"I heard a rumour you like boys," she whispered. "I like boys too. Maybe we can do something together."

"Like a threesome?" I was curious despite having no desire to have her anywhere near me. "Me, another dude, and you?"

"If you want. Would you like to take turns on me?"

"Not especially. If you're not down with watching me fuck another dude, it'd be the wrong party for all of us."

Her confusion was almost comical, but I wasn't the complete tosser I'd once been. I got nothing from being an arsehole. "Look," I tried again. "You're beautiful, and it's true, I like men as much as women, but I'm not up for a faceless fuck. We all deserve better, especially you."

The woman rolled her eyes and wandered off. Hacked off, I slumped against the wall and drank more Coke. My heart knew it was better than lacing myself with the coke of a different kind, but boredom made me twitchy. Freddie was like a pig in shit with girls all over him and probably wouldn't notice if I slipped away. *Do it. Go home. Or go back to Sam. Who cares if he's on the pull?*

I cared, obviously. And if there was one trait I'd retained from the father who wanted nothing to do with me now I wasn't a big shot football player, it was the stubbornness of a goddamn mule. I stayed where I was, leaning against the ornate wall, until the club emptied out and it was time to go home.

The Christmas feeling returned when I got back to the flat to find Sam already there.

He was asleep on the couch, fully dressed, right down to his battered Docs, his phone clutched in one hand, a half-drunk Kopparberg on the coffee table. I eyed the sickly sweet cider with distaste —*how can he drink that shit*?—but as someone who'd necked six bottles of Diet Coke, I couldn't really comment.

I considered unlacing his boots and wrangling him out of his coat. He slept like the dead, especially when he'd been on the shots, but that would've involved lifting him clean off the couch, and I didn't trust myself with something so precious. What if I woke him? Or worse, dropped him?

There was also the possibility that I'd carry him into my bedroom and lock the door, so I settled for covering him with a blanket and leaving him to it.

I'm so fucked.

5

Micah

My vaguely regular job as a personal trainer was the one thing in my life that helped me feel like a normal person. I wasn't naïve enough to believe my list didn't book up because of who I was, but I was picky about who I took on. At present, every client on my list was over sixty and wanted to train for no other reason than to feel better. I had zero interest in macros and gains, and I couldn't pretend. Not anymore.

I put Mr Vincenzo through his paces on the recumbent bike, stretched his old muscles out, and sent him home with a resistance band and a home-care plan. Then I hit the pool, eager to get my shit done so I could head home. At some point in the night, Sam had peeled himself from the couch and gone to bed. Uncharacteristically, he'd shut his bedroom door, denying me a glimpse of him before I'd left for work. I was craving my fix, but more than that, I missed him. Our library trip seemed a long time ago.

My body didn't always behave the way I wanted it to: specifically, my leg. The scarring was tight and vicious, and if I was the slightest bit dehydrated, brutal cramps triggered from my calf to my thigh. I was in the habit of taking care of myself to avoid bullshit like that, but a late night combined with a belly full of pop was to prove my undoing.

On my sixteenth length, pain hit me like a bullet train. The analysis was too close to home, but if I didn't want to drown, I didn't have time to deflect it.

I struggled to the edge of the pool and hauled myself out. My good leg held me up long enough to flop to a nearby lounger, but that was it. I was done and in so much pain I could've cried.

Cold set in. I wrapped my arms around myself and shivered, wishing I'd chosen the other side of the pool to collapse—the side where I'd left my towel. Thankfully, the gym was deserted this early on a Sunday, so there were no witnesses to my meltdown, but to be honest, I was fucked enough to ask for a hand up, a new skill I'd picked up in therapy. Shame there was no one around.

The pain in my leg, exacerbated by my inability to warm my damp skin, got worse. Muscle spasms twisted me up from my calf to my shoulder blades. An inhuman groan escaped me. Legit rolling back into the pool to drown myself seemed like the only solution, and I drove my fist into the lounger. Limping around like a dipshit, I could live with, but this? Creasing up in public when I'd already made a fool of myself enough for a thousand lifetimes? Yeah. I could've cried about that too.

"Micah?"

"Huh?" I ripped my eyes open. Of all people, Freddie stood over me, his frown one I recognised from a much darker time. "What?"

"Dude, what's wrong? Cramp?"

I nodded, gritting my teeth.

Freddie crouched beside me. He laid a tentative hand on my seized leg, and I hit the roof.

He retracted like he'd been burned. "Jesus. Okay, let's get you out of here."

Was he fucking mad? I fell back on the lounger and glared at him. "Just get me a towel, bro."

"On it."

Freddie produced a towel from seemingly nowhere, then a hoodie and a pair of sweats I had zero chance of pulling up my fucked leg on my own.

"Come on, mate," Freddie coaxed. "Help me out a little bit here."

Somehow, he got me dressed without me screaming or punching him in the face. The warmth from the clothes eased the spasms in my back, but my leg was still a write-off. I couldn't breathe. Freddie held a bottle of water to my lips. I choked on it and pushed it away. "Leave me. I'm fine."

"Yeah, and I'm a bird in a dress. Look, my car's right outside. Let me take you to a doctor."

"I don't need a doctor. It's cramp."

"So? Wouldn't hurt to get checked out *and* to get away from prying eyes. Know what I mean?"

I looked beyond him. The pool had started to fill with weekend gym wankers who never showed their faces during the week. None had noticed me and Freddie huddled in the corner yet, but it wouldn't be long. "I can't walk."

"I know. I'll help you. It's right outside, mate. I've got you."

I'd spent a lot of time wondering how Freddie could be such a dick to the rest of the world but an absolute dude for me, even after I'd fallen out of the closet. Especially after. But I couldn't think straight—*ha*—enough to argue with him now. This pain was fucking lit.

I took his outstretched hands and let him haul me to my feet.

I came to on a hospital bed in what looked like a hotel room. My head was fuzzy, and I was alone. A dull ache reverberated through my damaged leg, a fraction of the agony I last remembered before some quack in a white coat had stuck me with a needle. I tested it for movement, pleased to find the muscles loose enough to bend and stretch but horrified by the fact I had no trousers on beneath the thin white blanket. *What the fuck happened?*

"Muscle relaxants," Freddie said from somewhere before looming over me. "Then you fell asleep. Considering how cut up you were, I figured I'd leave you to wake up on your own."

The fact that he'd seen me in a far bigger mess than this didn't make his presence any less humiliating. "Where am I?"

"Fallgate Clinic. Liverpool Street."

My heart sank. Not because Freddie had spirited me to a private clinic without the goldfish bowl horrors of a public A&E, but because I had no idea how I was going to pay for it. I mean, I had money, but I needed that shit to last the rest of my entire goddamn life. "Fuck."

"You okay?"

"Yeah, man. Thanks for helping me out."

"You don't look too impressed. If you're worried about fronting the bill, don't. I got you."

"I can't let you do that."

"The fuck not? I've got more money than sense, remember?"

I had no counter for that. Looking at Freddie was sometimes like looking in a mirror fitted with a time machine. Except he wasn't the selfish fuckhead I'd been when I'd had the world at my feet. "I'll pay you back."

"Piss off."

I closed my eyes, drifting. "My brain hurts."

"I don't know why. Can't be all that big if you were stupid enough to go swimming with that leg after a late night in the city."

"I didn't drink."

"Nah, but you were still out late with no dinner."

"You sound like Sam," I murmured, despite his words echoing *my* thoughts from sometime earlier.

"Speaking of which," Freddie said. "I messaged him for you."

That got my attention. "You what?"

"I sent him a message request on Instagram letting him know you were with me and didn't have your phone. You know, in case he was wondering why you went to the gym and never came back."

"What time is it?"

"Half-two."

"Half *what?*"

I scrambled to get up, all jelly legs and flailing arms.

Freddie restrained me. "Easy. You can't go anywhere till the doc comes back and signs you off."

"I need to leave."

"Uh-huh. He won't be long."

"Fre—"

"Dude. Stop. You aren't walking out of here like this. Wait for the doc and I'll drive you."

Liverpool Street was a stone's throw from home. That I couldn't make it on my own was more humiliating than I was prepared to deal with. "I was supposed to be with Sam."

I spoke as much to myself as to Freddie, but he answered me anyway. "I know, mate. You told me in the car on the way over here. That's why I messaged him."

"What did you say?"

"That you were with me and you didn't have your phone."

"Did he reply?"

"Nope. But he might not see the message. We don't follow each other on social media."

My heart continued its merry way to the pit of my stomach. Sam spent as much time on social media as I did grocery shopping. There was zero chance he'd see that message unless he actively went looking for it, and why would he do that? As far as he was concerned, I was just the bozo who'd let him down. Again.

"I need to go home."

"Soon, mate. Soon."

Soon turned out to be two hours later, by the time my legs were working properly. Freddie dropped me outside the flat, and I limped upstairs like a deranged robot, despite knowing full well Sam would already be at work. That he'd have left thinking I didn't give a shit about him enough to let him know I wouldn't be there when he woke up.

I opened the door to two omelettes lying cold on the kitchen counter and a blank Post-it that might as well have had *fuck you* scribbled on it. Sam was the light and noise in my life. I needed him like I needed air. His absence in my life at this precise moment was killing me. Only a desperate need for more sleep kept me from dashing down the road to the pub.

Sometime later, a colleague from the gym dropped my bag off. Bleary eyed, I dug my phone out and charged it up to find a string of missed calls and messages from Sam, the last two sent in quick succession ten minutes before his shift had started.

Sam: *so . . . you either didn't make it to the gym and you're snoozing in bed, or you've stood me up. if you're in bed, know that i will wake u up with cold water*

Sam: *u stood me up? u better have a reason that's way hotter than my grimy self this morning*

Sam: *ok, now I'm worried. u ever think of texting ur roommate back so he doesn't have to wonder if u even came home last night?*

Sam: *forget it. got freddie fuckstick's message on insta. have a nice life :)*

The smiling emoji was the fucking death of me. Sam was a firecracker when his temper was high, but I'd lived with him long enough to know he was passive aggressive AF when he was upset. I'd seen him send heart-eye emojis to his ex rather than tell that douche to die in a fire and wish homophobic cockheads in the pub a good day rather than throat punch them.

I typed out a reply. Deleted it and started another, but words didn't seem enough. *Fuck it.* I chanced a shower and threw on some clothes. However pissed at me he was, I had to see him. Even if he told me to go fuck myself before I got the chance to explain, which was highly likely, because explaining myself to anyone had never come easy. Chances were, I'd stand in front of him like the idiot I was, and nothing would ever change.

6

Sam

Bad moods sucked the life out of me. When I was a kid, my mum had called me Sunshine Sam, but my light had dimmed as I'd got older and discovered cynicism. As an adult, I relied on sarcasm and expecting the worst, so anything better was a pleasant surprise.

I'm not sure what I'd expected from a day that had begun so craptastic, but Micah bursting into the pub in the middle of Sunday happy hour, looking like he'd been dragged through a hedge backwards, was not it. He also looked like he hadn't slept for a week, which concerned and irritated me in equal measure. When was I going to learn that worrying about him got me nowhere?

Not today, apparently, if the flare in my chest was anything to go by.

I finished serving my customer and searched out Céleste. She'd already clocked Micah, and she nodded to the alcove. "Take a break," she mouthed.

Grateful, I blew her a kiss, then shouldered my way to the door where Micah still stood, dark hair a riot, eyes rimmed with shadowy smudges. "What the hell are you doing?"

He blinked. "What?"

"You're blocking the door."

Micah didn't move. I grabbed his elbow and tugged him forwards. He stumbled. People stared. "Jesus. Are you on drugs?"

A ghost of a grin warmed his unusually pale face. "Not on purpose."

Bone-deep anger bloomed in my gut. Was he serious? Had he rocked up to my work off his nut just to piss me off?

I yanked his elbow again and towed him to the staff alcove. With him stashed away, I fetched him a Diet Coke and dumped it in front of him. "What the hell is wrong with you? First you don't come home at night without telling me, then you show up here buzzing your tits off. Are you trying to make me hate you?"

Another slow blink. "What are you talking about?"

"I'm talking about *you*, Micah. And how hanging out with Freddie turns you into an inconsiderate prick."

Micah stared. It was as if my words were coming too fast and he was struggling to process them.

Well, tough shit. He was an arsehole; at least, he was right now, in my opinion. Trouble was, he *wasn't*, and that's why I was so fucking angry with him. And at myself. It had been my idea for him to get out more. And look where it had got us: me screeching at him in a crowded pub while he came down from whatever wild night he'd had with his old mates. *How many times do you need to tell yourself you're not his fucking mother?*

Likely another seventy-five million. Especially as all I could think about was the fact that he probably hadn't eaten since we'd last shared a plate of marmite toast over the breakfast bar. I clearly didn't know him as well as I'd thought, but I knew hungry Micah when I saw him. "Wait here," I snapped. "I'll get you some food."

I barrelled off to the kitchen and fudged him a sandwich from the Sunday roast joints dotted around—chicken and pork with apple sauce and stuffing. I nearly scrounged up a bowl of potatoes too but spitefully changed my mind. *Real mature, sunshine.*

With heavy legs, I took the plate out to Micah and slid it in front of him.

He only had one eye open, and I wanted to shake him.

I settled for flopping onto the seat beside him. "Eat."

"I can't while you're still so mad at me."

"I'm not mad."

"Liar."

"I'm not a liar either. See?" I forced a smile that made my reluctant jaw ache. "Now eat your breakfast."

"It's six o'clock."

Like I needed him to remind me a whole day had passed since he hadn't shown up to eat breakfast and watch that stupid DVD with me. I'd got up assuming he was at the gym and had waited and waited like a chump until it became apparent he probably hadn't come home from his big dick night out. Freddie's gloating message had come through a millisecond before I'd seriously considered doing what roommates do when the other doesn't come home at night for the first time ever and aren't answering their phone. Boy, was I glad I hadn't done that. *Yeah, sorry, officer. I didn't realise my roommate actually is the flaky douchebag he said he was.*

Micah reached out and unclenched my fist. "I'm sorry I wasn't there."

"It's okay."

"It's not. I wanted to be, but—"

"Look, I get it, okay? You had a good night and you didn't fancy rolling home to watch some shitty movie adaptation with me. It's fine, Micah. It's not like it was a fucking date. I'm sure Freddie is *way* more fun than me."

"That's what you think happened? That I ditched you to party with Freddie?"

"Didn't you? Because he seemed pretty pleased with himself when he let me know you weren't dead this morning."

"Wow. You're so fucking clever if you got all that from his barely literate message. Last I heard, all he said was I didn't have my phone."

"Whatever. It doesn't matter."

"Sam."

"*What*?"

Micah gazed at me a moment longer, then something seemed to flicker in his troubled eyes. He shrugged and picked up his sandwich. "Nothing. Thanks for the breakfast."

Micah

Life had a way of monotonously carrying on when all I wanted was to stop the world and get off. To go back to the way things were before. To those precious few months where Sam had believed I was a better man. Or maybe he never had. Maybe he'd been waiting for me to fuck up all along.

You didn't fuck up. None of this was your fault.

But it was. Because my fuck-ups had started long before I'd met Sam, and everyone knew it. *He* knew it. How else would his first conclusion be that I'd spent all night banging coke with Freddie and sacked him off in the process?

What was laughable was that Freddie had never snorted a line in his life. He liked a posh drink and the attention of a beautiful woman, but he was more committed to the game than I had ever been.

At home, the storm passed. Sam gave me a wide berth for a few days, and I didn't seek him out. When he was home, I stayed in my room, and when he wasn't, I sulked on the couch. But eventually, our paths crossed and the silence broke. Normality returned, except it wasn't normal at all. The easiness of our friendship had gone. The banter. He stopped inviting me places, and I stopped pretending I didn't want to go.

It was murder. I took on more clients at the gym to keep busy. When that didn't work, I booked an extra session with the psychologist who'd rescued me from the psychiatric hospital. I was a world away from where I'd been back then, but I knew better than to let shit fester.

My psychologist was Meera, a Bangladeshi woman with kind eyes, beautiful hair, and a different necklace every time I saw her. It was once a month these days, but when I'd been seeing her every few days, her collection had fascinated me.

Today, she wore a copper chain studded with jade elephants. I stared at it for a while, before her patient questioning brought me to life.

"So, it's unsettled you to fall out with Sam. That's understandable. You've become good friends since you've lived together, yes?"

"Not on purpose," I started, but it was such an echo of the conversation I'd shared with Sam in the pub that I stopped and searched for new words. "We are friends, or at least we were before this. But I never meant to get close to him. I wanted to live with someone who got on with their own life and let me get on with mine."

"Why?"

"Because I wanted to be left alone. I had so much attention from the press, from doctors, arguments with my family. I just wanted to be . . . alone."

"Then why did you rent a flat with anyone at all. Why not *be* alone if that's what you truly wanted?"

"Because I was scared."

"Of what?"

"Of everything I just said."

It didn't make much sense, even to me, but Meera wrote it down all the same. "Tell me," she said. "Why have you continued to allow Sam to believe you took drugs the night you went out with Freddie? You said he thinks you didn't come home at all. But that's not what happened, so why haven't you told him the truth?"

It was a question I'd asked myself a thousand times since the scene in the alcove. Sam was hot-headed, but he was a listener. There was no sensible reason I couldn't have turned the conversation around. I'd chosen not to. I'd fucking *chosen* to let him believe I was an indifferent fuckhead. "I guess it's easier to let him down now rather than a year down the line when we have more to lose."

"More?"

"A longer friendship."

"Why are you so convinced you'd let him down? You don't owe him anything, Micah. If you make a mistake, there's no one it affects more than you. Also, Sam has been a loyal friend to you so far. What makes you think he wouldn't forgive you?"

And so it went on. Meera dissected my relationship with Sam until I didn't know which way was up. The only thing I was certain of was that I'd fucked it up by not telling him the truth about that night. I wasn't guilty of what he'd accused me of, but I was guilty, nonetheless.

I left only a little more grounded than when I'd arrived. As I always did after therapy, perhaps a test of sorts, I took the Tube home. It wasn't far, just two stops, but it was long enough for my brain to take a trip down memory lane. The track I'd got hurt on was miles from where I was right now, in every sense of the word. All tube trains smelt the same, though, and if I closed my eyes, I was right there, teetering on the edge of something I couldn't control. A despair so deep it had almost drowned me.

"Micah, were you trying to kill yourself?"

I'd always answered *no* to that question, but I'd yet to figure out what else I could've been doing. Maybe I never would.

And maybe it didn't matter.

The train pulled into Moorgate. I pulled my hood low over my face and braved the weekday commuter crowds, thankful this corner of the city was more concerned with stock markets than fragile ex-footballers. I dodged my way through the suited and booted until I reached the ancient building where Sam's grandparents had once lived. Out of habit, I checked the time to see if he'd be home. It was Thursday, and he usually spent them hunched up with his books on the couch, but when I let myself into the flat, he was in the hallway, a packed bag in his hand.

My heart dropped. "What are you doing?"

Sam fished his keys from the dish by the front door without looking at me. "I'm going to stay with my parents."

"Why?"

"Because they're my parents, and I haven't seen them since Christmas."

It was February, and his parents had been in town two weeks ago. I'd seen them. He'd seen them. The whole fucking world had seen them—his parents were the life and soul of the party. "*Why*?"

"Don't do this."

"Do what? Ask you why you're running out on me when you've barely spoken for a week?"

"Not everything is about you."

"Never said it was. Just that *this* is. I know it. So you could at least look me in the face and tell me."

"Tell you what? That I feel awkward as fuck in my own home? Because if you haven't figured it out yet, you're more dense than I thought."

He still wasn't looking at me. And he spoke quietly, but his words cut deep. This was his home more than mine. If he wasn't comfortable here, I was the one who should be packing my bags.

I had nowhere to go. I pictured Freddie's Kensington loft and wanted to die. That shit wasn't me. Never had been. My quiet life with Sam was so fucking precious to me. I couldn't lose it. I couldn't lose *him*. "Sam, please."

Exasperation rolled off his hunched shoulders in waves. He turned to face me, jaw set, but the second our eyes met, something—everything—changed. He sucked in a shaky breath and held out his free hand. "Come with me."

7

Sam

My trip to my parents' house was supposed to have been an escape from Micah. Not literally from him, but the angst that came from sharing a space with someone you wanted to love on and throttle all at the same time. But his stricken face had broken me. I couldn't leave him.

So I took him with me.

We caught a north-bound train out of King's Cross. My parents' home was four hours away, but I liked trains. With my grandparents living in London, I'd spent most school holidays trundling from Yorkshire and back again. The rocking motion soothed me. Even the smell of musty upholstery was nostalgic.

I had no idea what Micah was thinking. He was still clutching my hand an hour after he'd gripped it so tight in the hallway. I had no inclination to let him go, but at the same time, I had no idea what it meant. How I felt about Micah wasn't new. It was the intensity I couldn't swallow. The uncertainty. I had *no idea* how he felt about *anything*, let alone me. Was he holding my hand because he wanted to? Or because he was drowning?

Either way, I wasn't letting go.

"How many trains is it?"

Micah's gruff voice startled me out of my thoughts. "Two, and a bus. This one to York, then onto Scarborough. We get the bus from there into Whitby."

"That's long, man."

"Well, we could have flown EasyJet to Manchester, but that's a little extreme, don't you think?"

His grunt was noncommittal, and he went back to watching goal clips on his phone, funnily enough, of his old team based in Manchester, a time in his life he seemed to cling to whenever he talked about football. He never mentioned his short-lived stint in London before the catastrophic injuries to his leg had ended his career for good, and I never asked why. I rarely asked anything of him aside from what he wanted for dinner.

Perhaps I should have. Maybe if he found it easier to talk to me, we wouldn't be where we were right now.

We changed trains in York and travelled an hour to Scarborough. Then it was another hour on the bus. Micah fell asleep leaning against the window . . . still holding my hand. No one around us had noticed. Not that I cared. If anyone gave Micah a wrong look, I'd deck them.

I roused him at our final stop and helped him off the bus, much to his obvious displeasure.

"I can walk, you know."

"Well, you don't have to. My parents live over there." I turned him towards the old town nestling by the harbour. "The white house."

"By the pub?"

"Of course. You've met my parents, right?"

He grinned a little. He'd met my raucous parents a few times and always, *always* in the Fox when they'd been passing through on a knees up. "You said they weren't like that at home."

"They're not. But the pub isn't their home, and that's where they spend most of their time. Come on."

"They know I'm coming with you, don't they?"

"Of course. I messaged my mum while we were still in London. She went out and got an extra sack of potatoes."

Micah's eyes widened.

I laughed. Couldn't help it. "Oh, you sweet city boy. Hope you weren't planning on watching your carb intake while we're here."

"I didn't plan anything at all."

"Even better." I slung my bag over my shoulder and towed him towards my parents' house. It was a large cottage on the outskirts of the old town with amazing views of the harbour. As a child, I'd spent hours watching the sea roll in and out and imagining how I'd escape the village by boat and travel to far-flung lands. I'd got as far as London in the end, and I was happy with that, but occasionally I found myself wondering what would have become of me if I'd stayed. *Nothing. You'd be pulling pints in a different pub.*

Valid.

My parents weren't home. They'd made up the spare room for Micah, a double bedroom in the extension on the side of the house that was accessed through an adjoining door in my childhood pit.

Micah finally released my hand and flexed his fingers. "This is your room?"

"*Was* my room. I moved to London when I was eighteen."

"Leaving your Batman poster behind."

"Hey, I had a thing for Christian Bale. Sue me."

Micah said nothing. He drifted closer to the poster and stared at it. I wondered who had been his first man-crush and then felt like shit. I'd lived the perfect gay life in my teens. Coming out to my parents had been easy, hilarious, even, and they'd had my back ever since. The poster had been a gift from my mum when she'd caught me with a dodgy magazine and a sock. Micah's parents hadn't spoken to him since the tabloids had yanked him out of the closet, and however indifferent he acted about it, I knew it hurt. Still. Always.

I poked my head into the room that would be his for however long he was here—somehow, we hadn't discussed it. Just thrown his clothes in a bag and jumped on a train. And now here we were in my mum's house. *How is this even my life?*

Downstairs, the front door opened and closed.

Micah flinched and sucked in a breath.

I found his hand again and gave it a brief squeeze. "It's okay. They don't bite. You can hang out up here if you want, though. I'll tell them you're asleep."

"Right. Cos I'm not enough of a wet blanket already."

"What the fuck does that mean?"

He shrugged. "Nothing. Just bitching."

"So . . . you're coming downstairs?"

"Of course."

Bemused, I led him downstairs to my parents' cosy kitchen. It had terracotta tiles, an AGA, and an ancient chip pan that my dear old dad was already cranking up.

My mum—Loraine—greeted me with a hug that squashed my bones. "You're too skinny," she chided. "And you." She gave Micah the same treatment. "You kids can't survive on avocados, you know."

"I literally can't remember the last time I ate one, Mum, and Micah hates them."

"It's true," Micah said. "I'd rather have bacon."

"You'll like your tea then. Bob's doing gammon and chips."

Micah's face brightened. "With the crispy eggs that Sam makes?"

"Of course. Flaming Nora, you two are so domesticated it makes my heart bleed."

I opened my mouth to correct her, but the words died in my throat. What was the point? My mum, never one to pick holes in me about how my life was going, had already moved on to the fridge to retrieve a jumbo pack of gammon steaks from the butcher up the road and heave a sack of potatoes from the cupboard under the stairs. I hadn't been joking when I'd warned Micah about his carb intake over the next few days.

Could he handle it?

Time would tell.

"Your parents put me in a coma." Micah flopped on the bed and rubbed his stomach. "Do they always eat like that?"

"Yup. I'm surprised my dad hasn't had a heart attack."

"Maybe it's the Northern blood."

"I don't think cholesterol is that discerning." I ventured further into the room and hovered like an awkward bee, unwilling to leave him alone but unsure of my place in my parents' spare room. "What do you want to do tomorrow?"

"Tomorrow?"

"Yeah, unless you wanted to go home?"

Micah sat up on his elbows. "I don't want to go home, but I gotta ask, how long were you planning on staying? You know, before I gate-crashed your great escape."

I mourned the lightness we'd once enjoyed, when nothing except what we were having for dinner had mattered. *How did we fuck this up so royally in such a short space of time?* I wished I knew. Giving in to the urge to be closer to him, I sat on the edge of the bed. "I took a week off work."

"A week?"

"Yeah."

"And you weren't going to tell me? You were just gonna go?"

"Are you taking the piss? Maybe I'd have got one of my mates to text you on my behalf a couple of days later. That's how it works, isn't it?"

"If you say so."

"Don't do that."

Micah sighed. "Do what?"

"Imply that I've invented the narrative."

That earned me another sigh, and I wanted to shake him, hard, until all his shutters fell down and how he really felt shone through. "Can I ask you something?"

Wariness crept into Micah's dark gaze. "Go on . . ."

"Why did you do it?"

"Do *what*?"

"Go out with Freddie and get so fucked up."

"Who said I did?"

"What?"

Micah tilted his head sideways. "Tell me when, in your version of events, *anyone* told you I wasn't home when you got up because I'd been on the sniff with Freddie. In fact, tell me when *you* decided I didn't come home that night at all, because that still doesn't make sense to me."

I stared. "What are you trying to say?"

"I'm not trying to say anything. I'm asking you a question."

"It's two questions."

"Whatever. Answer them."

I turned his words over in my head, disquiet building in my gut as I realised he had a gargantuan point. I'd thrown accusations at him based on my assessment of his appearance and my dislike for a friend from his old life who always seemed to be tugging him backwards. In . . . my opinion. Which didn't mean shit without facts.

Facts that weren't there. "Was I wrong?"

"About what?"

"Any of it. All of it."

Micah blew out yet another heavy breath. "Yeah. You were."

"For all of it?"

His answering silence was deafening. "Jesus fucking Christ, why didn't you *tell* me? And what the hell did happen? You've never gone MIA like that. At least, not with me. Before I got Freddie's message, I was fucking terrified."

"Freddie figured. That's why he sent it."

"Why were you still with him?"

"I wasn't still with him. I was with him *again*. We go to the same gym, remember? I see him on random days all the time."

Gym. Freddie. Missing puzzle pieces began to click into place, accompanied by a heavy dose of mortification. It hadn't for a single second occurred to me that Micah had come home and gone out again while I'd slept. "What happened with him? Where was your phone?"

Micah cringed. "At the gym. My leg cramped in the pool and I couldn't walk. Freddie scooped me up and dragged me to some quack in Liverpool Street. They gave me some shots that knocked me out. By the time I woke up, it was late. I came to find you as soon as I was properly conscious, but—"

"But I ripped your head off."

"A bit."

I covered my face with my hands. "I'm so sorry. Why didn't you tell me I was being a prick?"

Micah shifted on the bed. Warm fingers wrapped around my wrists and tugged my hands away. "Because you weren't being a prick. You were judging me by everything I've done in the past, and I deserved that."

"No, you didn't!" My voice rose loud enough that my mum would definitely hear me if I couldn't keep a lid on it. "You've never done anything to me. What right did I have to say such vile things to you based on some bullshit I'd seen in *The Sun*?"

"Every right. People should've said that shit to me years ago. Maybe if they had, I might've got through that time in my life without making such a fucking mess."

"Micah, you were in an impossible situation. There are no openly queer players in the Premier League. Not one. There never has been. And look what happened to Dominic Ramos when he came out? He had to retire, like, in the same breath. I know you didn't want to do that."

"Had to anyway, though, didn't I? Cos I fucked it up. And, if I hadn't been such a basket case in the first place, I'd never have got caught."

"So you would've lived in the closet forever?"

Micah hissed through his teeth the way he so often did when he was frustrated. "I don't know, man. Maybe. Or maybe I could've waited until I was done playing. Cos I wasn't done. Nowhere fucking near."

Sadness eclipsed the shame building in my blood. "I'm sorry you lost your dream."

"'S not your fault."

"But this is." I gestured between us. "God, I'm such an arsehole."

Micah rolled his eyes. "For fuck's sake. How can that be even remotely true when I had every opportunity to set you straight? It's not like I gave you a chance, is it? I let you think whatever came into your mind when you looked at me."

"Why?"

"Because it suited me better than admitting I can't swim up and down some dinky hipster pool without losing my shit. For real, Freddie had to dress me at the side of the pool like a fucking baby."

"You're lucky he was there."

"I am. I need you to stop giving him such a hard time. I know he acts like a goon when he's out, but he's not like that, really. He's never touched drugs in his life. Or cheated on his girlfriends. He's a good bloke."

After the tale Micah had told me tonight, I was starting to believe it, but Freddie was the last thing on my mind. All I could think about was the fact that Micah had been in so much pain he'd needed a doctor, and my only response had been to tear him apart. "I'm sorry I'm such a shit friend."

"Fuck off, mate."

"It's true," I protested.

"No, it's not. I didn't tell you the truth, and I know you only reacted that way because you care. The only question for me is why."

"Why what?"

"Why do you care so much about me? I'm a fuckwit, Sam. Always have been, even without football culture."

"You're not a fuckwit."

"I am. I'm caught up in my own head all the time, and I don't think the way I should. Freddie sent you that message of his own accord. I forgot all about my phone until he told me."

And I forgot about you. He didn't say it, but he didn't have to. "You were in a lot of pain, and by the sound of it, off your nut on whatever drugs they gave you. It's understandable that an omelette date with me wasn't your first priority."

"But—"

"Just stop, okay? It's fine. I was a prick to you, and I'm so fucking sorry. I let—" Fuck. Was I really going to do this? "I let my feelings for you get in the way of being your friend."

"Your feelings for me?"

"Yeah. I like you, Micah . . . way too much. But I know you don't feel that way about me, and I totally accept that. I want to be your friend, a *good* friend, and I'm so sorry my ego got in the way of that."

"Are you done?"

"Yup. But don't say a word." I scrambled off his bed. "Don't say anything, please? I promise I'll be a normal person in the morning. I gotta go. Night."

"Sam—"

I fled the room without letting him speak, and the irony wasn't lost on me that it was how we'd got into this mess in the first place. But I had to go. I couldn't face him blunting his usual sharp tongue with forced diplomacy as he tried to let me down gently. He didn't need to do it any more than I had needed to spill my guts to him in the first place.

Shame that thought came way too late.

I flopped down on my own bed. For a moment, I imagined I heard him get up and shuffle across the carpet, but it was all in my head. Silence was my only companion.

Tired, I undressed and crawled into bed. The sheets smelt of the same lavender fabric conditioner we used at home, and I hoped perhaps the smell would help Micah settle. He'd told me before he didn't sleep well in new places. That away games had often left him so sleep deprived he could barely kick the ball straight. His confession had explained why he'd paced our living room every night for the first two weeks he'd lived with me, his leg dragging behind him. Now it made my heart ache so bad I knew I'd be awake forever.

It was two in the morning when his text came through.

Micah: *stop making assumptions about how i feel*

8

Micah

I woke with a jump to textured wallpaper and a bed that smelt like good dreams. Not that I'd had any dreams. One moment I'd been staring at my phone screen, the next it had been, well, now.

The house was deadly quiet. I rolled over and scowled at my blank phone screen. I'd stayed awake for hours hoping Sam would respond to my cryptic non-message, but he hadn't. And why the hell would he? It wasn't as if I'd confessed that I liked him way too much too. And now it was arse o'clock in the morning and I was awake once again to be all up in my feelings.

Awesome.

My bladder drove me out of bed. I opened the door like a ninja, but there was no need; Sam's bed was empty.

The bathroom was at the end of the hall. The floorboards creaked beneath my feet and I cringed with every step until I made it. I took a piss and contemplated returning to the unfamiliar bedroom that somehow smelt like home. I was bone-tired, but not knowing where Sam was sent anxiety dancing through my veins, and I knew I wouldn't find rest again until I'd found him.

I shuffled downstairs, half expecting to find his parents in the kitchen, still frying chips, but there was no one about. I poked around in the maze of quirky rooms, one after the other, wincing each time a door hinge whined, which was every fucking time. The last room was a den in the downstairs section of the extension—a small room with a patchwork couch and a flat-screen TV. Sam was curled up under a blanket watching an old episode of *ER* on mute.

"You realise Dr Kovac is only hot when he opens his mouth, right?"

Sam snapped his gaze to me, eyes wide. "Fuck. I didn't hear you come down. Everything okay?"

I limped to the couch and perched on the arm. "Yeah. Just woke up in a strange place, you know?"

"I know."

Of course he did. Sam listened to me when I spoke and remembered everything I told him. Because he cared. Because he liked me as much as I liked him. More. Maybe. Who the fuck knew?

My head was spinning. I slid over the arm of the couch and landed beside him. "I'm too messed up to be what you want."

It wasn't what I'd meant to say, not even close. But it was the truth.

Sam closed his eyes briefly and shook his head. "You're not too fucked up for *anything*."

"Dude, I have to take pills to get out of bed in the morning, I can't sleep, I can't figure out if how I feel on any given day is real or a side effect of that shit, and the only thing I'm good for is training geriatrics."

Sam flinched as if the influx of negativity was too much for him and it would take a moment for him to unpick it. "You take medication because you've been hurt. That doesn't make you unworthy of living. Besides, I already told you what I want is to be your friend, which I kind of thought we were already doing until I messed it up by passing judgement on a situation I knew nothing about."

"That wasn't your fault."

"Yes, it was."

We'd been over this already, and the mere thought of rehashing it made me want to die. I knocked my head on the back of the couch. "Whatever. My point is that however you think you feel about me, I'm not fucking worth it."

"However I think I feel about you." Sam's tone was deadpan but dangerous. "Look, I'm not going to argue with you about that, cos I know I'll never win while you see yourself the way you do. Just know that I really am sorry, okay? For everything that's happened over the last few weeks. I should've had a better handle on things, and I didn't."

Frustration boiled up inside me. My heart was screaming at me to tell him that everything coming out of my dumb-fuck mouth was a world away from how I really felt. That I'd been enchanted by him from the moment we'd met. But the words wouldn't come. It was like I had an iron curtain between my brain and my soul, and the ache in my heart was my trapped emotions trying to escape. "It's not your fault."

"How's your leg?"

"What?"

"Your leg." Sam sat up. "You never told me if it was better."

"It's fine."

"Really?"

I shrugged. "Mostly. It still feels a bit . . . weird, but it doesn't hurt any more than it usually does. It cramped so bad because I was tired and dehydrated. I shouldn't have swum so hard."

"You should've skipped the pool and come home for your breakfast, huh?"

"Yup. See? My fault, not yours."

Sam snorted. The fatigue in his face told me he was as tired of this conversation as I was, but there was humour too—the dry, self-deprecating wit that had drawn me to him in the first place. "It's four o'clock in the morning. Do you want to go back to bed?"

With you? Yes. By myself, no thanks. I shook my head. "I'm up now."

"Up for walking?"

"Where?"

"You'll see."

I stood at the sea wall, huddled in my coat with the hood up. "It's cold."

Sam laughed and pulled me closer to the edge, so the waves sprayed my face. It wasn't the same as getting wet, more like a ghost from the sea had walked across my skin. I liked it, but it was still fucking cold.

I turned away from the angry water and focussed on Sam. He seemed lighter now we were out of the house and away from the weight of our latest loaded conversation. Like the Sam I'd always known. His eyes were soft, his hair screwed up by the wind. He looked like I'd fucked him seven ways from Saturday, if we lived in the world that existed behind that damn curtain.

We started walking again, this time back inland, leaving the raging ocean behind. I missed it already. "I've never been that close to the sea before."

Sam cast me a sideways glance. "Seriously? But you've been all over the world playing football."

"On planes, coaches, and on the pitch. I never went exploring."

"What about when you were a kid? Holidays and stuff."

"Never went. My dad worked seven days a week and my mum was hooked on Valium, so she never left the house."

"You've never told me that."

"Which bit?"

"Any of it. You never talk about your family."

"I don't think they talk about me either."

Sam kicked a smooth rock. It skittered along the cobbled pavement until it collided with a lamppost. "It's really fucking shitty that they disowned you when you came out. That's some archaic fuckery."

He always used the best words. Sometimes I tried to keep up, but my limited vocabulary always showed me up in the end. "To be fair, I think it was more about the game than the orgy thing. Playing football was the only thing I ever did that they could be proud of.

Without it, I'm just the idiot that would've been kicked out of school if the academy hadn't snapped me up."

Sam grumbled under his breath. It shouldn't have been funny, but I grinned a little anyway. I loved it when he got ragey about stuff, even if that stuff was my clusterfuck of a personal life, and the cold wind was making my limp a hundred times worse than it ever was in the city.

I spotted a café up ahead, the kind that served filthy breakfasts and builder's tea. I grabbed Sam's arm and pointed. "I'm hungry."

He nodded and took my arm, guiding me around a bus stop and inside. I didn't need his help to stay upright, but I couldn't deny his fingers wrapped around my elbow felt almost as good as holding his hand. So I covered his hand with my own.

Surprised coloured Sam's gaze. He glanced between our hands and my face in rapid succession while I stared resolutely ahead. I didn't give a fuck. I might've been piss-poor at verbalising anything beyond a couple of curse words, but now I knew how this felt, I couldn't give it up.

We sat at a table by a condensation-soaked window. The bloke serving the tea and frying the bacon gave us a long look as he delivered our tray, but I couldn't decide if it was because he recognised me and/or Sam or the fact that two dudes holding hands freaked him out. And I didn't care about that either, until I had to let go of Sam to let him eat. I watched him squeeze brown sauce into his bacon roll. "So it's true. Northerners really do eat that crap. You have ketchup at home. Who are you putting on a show for?"

Sam licked his fingers.

He licked his fucking fingers.

"I'm not putting on a show. I guess I have different tastes depending on my environment. When I was a kid, I only ate ketchup with pie and mash when my granddad took me out. Up here, it's brown sauce all the way. Always has been."

"But brown sauce is disgusting."

"It's really not."

"It really is."

And just like that, our easy banter was back. Stress faded. He was Sam, I was Micah, and together we were two idiots who bumbled through life together under the same roof. 'Cept, of course, I was an actual idiot, and he was a fucking masterpiece of a human being.

We ate in comfortable silence. Under the table, his knee barely brushed the thigh of my bad leg. My scars throbbed, but for once not with the burn of simply existing, but with the excitement of his unwitting touch. It was a strange sensation, kind of like holding my breath for no reason. But I clung to it all the same.

When we were done, it was time to go back. Sam had plans to help his dad at work, and I, the interloper, had plans to do absolutely nothing. I had workout schedules for my new clients I could've worked on, but my brain felt too mushy. I wanted to take the reclaimed peace I'd found with Sam and savour it for a while.

We were outside his parents' house when he trailed to a stop. I mirrored him, naturally. "What's up?"

Sam turned to face me. We hadn't held hands since the café; the moment had passed. Again. But he reached for both of my hands now and gripped them so tight my knuckles clicked. "I just wanted to say thanks."

"To who?"

"To you, idiot, for this morning. For a while there, I was terrified we'd never get back to normal, you know?"

Normal. Was he kidding me? We were holding hands outside his parents' house in a place that was a world away from our city life. Even when we eventually went home, every instinct I had told me that nothing between us would ever be the same. As if knowing how Sam felt about me had altered my DNA, and I wouldn't be whole until I was worthy of whatever the fuck that meant.

9

Sam

I came back from my dad's plumbing shop to find Micah asleep on the couch in the den. My mum had covered him with a blanket and was creeping around the kitchen like a serial killer.

"I didn't want to wake him," she said.

I rolled my eyes and flicked her radio on, tuning it to her usual community station and setting the volume just below deafening. "Don't worry about that. He's a light sleeper, but only when it's too quiet."

"How do you know that?"

"Because I live with him, Ma. How do you think?"

My mum fished a jumbo tray of sausages out of the fridge. "I think there's an odd dynamic between you two if you're not having a bit of how's your father when no one's looking."

"You think we should be doing it when people *are* looking?"

"Give over." Loraine cuffed me upside the head. "You know what I mean."

I did, and it was so painfully close to the truth—and yet a lifetime away from it—that I wanted to stick my head in her chip pan. "We're not *doing* anything. We're friends, like we've always been."

"Doesn't seem like it the way he stares at you all the time. I wondered if that's why you'd brought him . . . to tell us you were together."

"Nope. Definitely not. He came because he needed a break from the city. You know he's had a hard time."

"Does his leg still give him trouble?"

I shrugged. "He doesn't talk about it much, but he has super bad days sometimes, and I've made them worse recently by being a dick about some stuff that isn't his fault."

It was as much as I was prepared to admit, but my mum was a mind reader, so they were wasted words anyway. She knew I liked him. Loved him, even. The pity in her eyes as she brewed me hot, sweet tea said it all.

She thunked the mug on the table with a quiet sigh. "Listen, son. I usually keep my mouth shut when it comes to my kids' lives, but let me say this—"

"Mum, please don't. Micah's complicated, okay? He doesn't—"

"Christ, child. Let me speak."

I pursed my lips, half-amused by her outrage and half-terrified of her rare wisdom, and nodded for her to continue.

Loraine sucked her teeth and went on. "You're right. That boy is complicated, so don't spend however long it takes thinking you know what's going on in his head. Let him breathe and find himself again so he can find you."

I'd rolled my eyes so much when I was a kid that my dad had accused me of trying out for the ocular Olympics. As an adult, I'd tried to rein it in, but all that meant right now was that my mum's words penetrated far deeper than they might've if I'd been distracted by being an insolent twat. "*. . . however long it takes . . .*" What did that even mean? That she genuinely saw something between me and Micah that we didn't? Or that she knew me well enough to guess that I'd screwed things up by putting words in his mouth?

As movement in the den reached me, I realised it didn't matter.

Whatever happened, I was in love with my roommate, and when did that end well for anyone not in a shitty rom-com script?

I don't think Micah had ever been hugged so much. For reasons my mum kept to herself, she'd taken to embracing him at every opportunity, often at moments when the rest of the world, including him, least expected it. I also didn't believe he'd ever eaten or slept so much. For days, it seemed as though he'd no sooner woken up than my parents were feeding him into another carb-induced coma.

When he wasn't eating or sleeping, I dragged him out to walk in the wind and the rain. Despite him complaining for ninety per cent of the time he was outside, I was pretty confident that he loved it, which was ironic, considering both him *and* my know-it-all mother had warned me off making assumptions about how he felt.

With that in mind, on our last day up north, I took him to the pub, hoping a couple of pints of paint-stripping ale would calm the anxious, overthinking monster in my head. "Diet Coke, right? Though I think it's Pepsi in here."

Micah cast another wary glance around my parents' favourite boozer. "Nah. I'll have what you're having."

"You want a pint of Old Peculiar?"

"Sure. Why not?"

"Okay." I bought two pints and slid one along the bar to him, ignoring the curious gaze of the server. Everyone round these parts knew my parents and likely remembered me, but Micah's face was probably familiar to them too, and for less pleasant reasons. Unless, of course, they recognised him as the incredible footballer he'd once been. It was goddamn criminal that his ten-year career had been mostly erased by his private life.

Micah ignored the server too. He took a sip of the dark ale in his glass and winced. "Wow. That's some moody shit."

I laughed. "This from the man who puts mayonnaise in steak sandwiches? Give me a break."

"What's wrong with that?"

"Everything."

"Weirdo."

"Shut up and drink your beer."

Micah took another braver swallow of his drink, this time without the full-body cringe. Just.

I sighed and led him to a table on the other side of the pub to the one where my parents usually sat. Eyes followed us, and a couple of fellas whispered to each other and tapped at their phones, clearly googling Micah's face.

He didn't seem to notice. Or, if he did, he had the best poker expression in the world. But then, this was his life. He didn't get papped as much as he had when we'd first met, but it still happened often enough for me to want to send *The Sun* a letter bomb.

Metaphorically speaking, obviously.

"So . . ." Micah trailed a fingertip around the rim of his glass. "I like your parents."

"You liked them before. I was worried the full-on experience would put you off."

"Why?"

"You like a quiet life."

"I *have* a quiet life. That ain't quite the same thing."

"What would your life be like if you could choose? Like, living the dream scenario here."

Micah drank more beer. "Not that different. Just maybe . . . I dunno. I guess I just want to be free, from myself and everything else."

"How so?" I knew I was poking a hornet's nest, but it had been so long since Micah had let his guard down that I couldn't stop.

And if he minded, it didn't show. Or perhaps the booze was loosening the tight hold he usually kept on himself. He leaned forwards, elbows on the table, and fixed me with a gaze that seemed to stop time. "If my brain didn't hold me hostage and some cockhead from *The Daily Mail* wasn't over there filming us, maybe I'd be able to just fucking tell you how much I want to kiss you right now."

He'd have surprised me less if he'd grown a unicorn horn and wings. "What?"

"You heard."

"I did, but I'm not sure it was real."

Micah grunted as if he said that kind of shit to me all the time. "It was real—it *is* real—but don't ask me to do anything about it because I don't know how. And it scares me . . . all of it, cos I need you in my life the way you always have been. I can't— Fuck."

He stopped and blinked hard. I started to reach for his hand, but the presence of a camera behind me stopped me in my tracks, and with a kick to the gut, I suddenly understood what he meant. How every move was a reality check of shattered privacy. I nudged his foot under the table. "Go on. I'm listening."

Micah sighed. "I know. You always listen, and that's what I'm talking about. If I messed everything up by throwing myself at you, I could lose that, and I just fucking can't. You're my best friend. I-I need you."

My head reeled from the influx of information. I struggled to process it, to not focus on the fact that he wanted to throw himself at me—*kiss me*—and unpick what he was actually trying to say. "Micah, nothing could ever happen that would stop us being friends. I'm here for you, okay? In whatever capacity you need me."

"What if I never figure what that is?"

"Then we carry on as we are. Nothing ever has to change. We're all right, aren't we?"

"You are." Micah drained his glass. "I'm a fucking lightweight. That dark shit has gone straight to my head."

I fought hard not to wonder if his uncharacteristic drinking had done more talking than his heart. Which turned out to be easier than I'd imagined, as tipsy Micah was adorable. I emptied my glass too and nodded at the bar. "Want another?"

"Fuck it. Why not?"

I could think of plenty of reasons, but none stuck, so I got up and fetched more beer from the bar. When I got back to Micah, he was scrolling through Instagram. He turned the screen to face me. "Do you know how many Premiership players followed me before the Grindr thing?"

"Um . . . no? The only players I can ever remember are Freddie and Dom Ramos, and that's only because he got outed too."

"They're good players to know, but my point is, like, hundreds of players followed me before, and now I reckon I've lost more than half of them."

"They dropped you?"

"Not straight away, but yeah, over time they've disappeared. Only a couple ever publicly acknowledge me. It's fucked up, right?"

"It's *wrong*. That's why I hate football. It generates all this wealth, but it's stuck in the dark ages when it comes to equality. I suppose the romantic in me thought things were changing, but they're not."

Micah shook his head. "To be fair, it's not just homophobia. The black dudes I played with are still getting bananas thrown at them, even in this country."

"That's sick."

"I know. But it's not my world anymore, so I guess it's someone else's problem."

"If you really thought that, you wouldn't give a crap how many Insta followers you have."

"I don't give a crap . . . anymore. I just thought it was interesting that none of them had the balls to disassociate themselves straight away and own their bullshit."

I could think of more colourful terms for it, but Micah didn't need my opinion on the state of the beautiful game or my opinion on Instagram. I was still enjoying his beer-loose tongue, though. And his closeness as he hunched ever further over the table. My skin tingled as heat seemed to radiate between us. I wished with all my heart that things were different, that I could close the distance between us and brush my lips over his. But if this was all we had forever, I'd take it. Micah was *my* best friend, and I needed him as much as he needed me.

We finished our drinks and escaped the pub before the temptation to buy more overcame me. Getting drunk with Micah was appealing for many reasons, but he didn't get wasted anymore, and I didn't want to be responsible for him hating himself in the morning.

I also didn't want either of us to forget our convoluted conversations. I needed him to remember for the rest of his life that I'd always be there for him. And I needed to remember for the rest of my own that there'd been a wonderful, surreal moment when he'd wanted to kiss me. No hangover in the world was worth losing that.

We took a walk before heading back to my parents' house. Micah had fallen in love with the sea, despite bitching about the cold. He stood at the sea wall and watched the stormy waves, his dark gaze dancing before he closed his eyes and leaned forwards, catching the spray in his face.

In that moment, he was so beautiful I wanted to weep. I could accept him not wanting to explore his feelings for me, but I couldn't live with him believing *he* wasn't worth it.

My hand closed around his arm before I knew what I was doing. He turned easily in my grasp, as if he'd expected my touch, and faced me. His lips moved, but no words came out. I traced my thumb over his bottom lip. He caught my wrist in a death hold but didn't stop me. I stepped closer, drawn to him with impossible force. Irresistible. "Micah."

"What, Sam? What do you want from me?"

"This," I whispered. "Just once."

I kissed him with the barest brush of my mouth over his. It was light as air, but the impact was like a speeding bullet. Breath left my lungs. I shuddered, shook my head, and pulled away.

But Micah still held my wrist in his vice-like grip. He yanked me back. Our chests collided and his gaze was fierce and velvet. "That's not fair."

"What isn't?"

"That you got to kiss me without knowing I ain't never put my lips on a bloke before you."

With my brain addled by his closeness, it took me a moment to compute his words. "You've never kissed a boy?"

"Nah. I wasn't into it. And I only ever kissed girls I thought I had actual feelings for. But, dude, you should know, I've had all-night dreams about kissing you."

My legs felt weak. Without Micah holding me up, I'd have crumpled to the ground. "In your dreams, how did it go?"

"Like this."

Micah kissed me, and it was light years away from the feather-light brush of lips I'd bestowed on him. He crushed us together, wrapping his arms around me in an embrace so tight and warm I couldn't see how it could ever end. He drove his tongue into my mouth, searching, probing, his hands rough as they moved to my face.

A moan escaped me. I tangled my fingers in his short hair, desperate for purchase, but as the kiss went on and on and on, I found nothing to tie me down to the world. I was flying, and the prospect of crash-landing belonged to someone else.

10

Micah

"You want almond milk or regular?"

I stared at Sam like I had every morning he'd asked me that question for the last week. Every long-arse day since we'd shuffled home from his parents' place up north. Whitby had been a surreal experience, but nowhere near as much as this—the eight a.m. stand-off when Sam got up and acted as though our great escape hadn't happened.

It was beyond my brain to accept that he was behaving exactly how he'd promised he would: he was my friend, and nothing had changed. Because *fuck me*, everything had changed. Now, as I watched him make porridge with the almond milk I'd jerked my head at, I wasn't pondering its protein content or ignoring the fact that I had to leave the flat three times today to be a functioning adult. Instead, I was entranced by the fragment of bottom lip caught between his teeth and his deft hands. Reason told me this wasn't new, that I'd been obsessed with him since day one, but kissing him had driven all reason away. Was it too much to wish we'd never come home?

"*Micah.*"

My internal monologue—which, to be honest, was boring even me—trailed off. Sam was scowling at me like a dude who'd said my name more than once. "Hmm?"

He rolled his eyes and slid a bowl of porridge loaded with bananas, honey, and seeds across the counter. "Eat your breakfast. Come on, I've got to get to college. I haven't got time to spoon-feed you."

It was a joke he'd made a thousand times before, and my reaction was always the same. I scooped porridge onto my spoon and flicked it at him. He laughed like the sun and ducked out of the way.

When the threat was gone, he came around the counter and stood beside me. He was dressed for the day while I was still scruffing it in my sweats. His jeans were, as ever, sinfully tight, and his black T-shirt was rolled up at the sleeves, revealing more of his sinewy biceps than I could cope with. "I've got to go," he said, apparently oblivious to the effect he was having on me. "I'm going straight to work after. Are you coming down tonight?"

"To the pub?"

"No, to the hair salon I work at. Of course I mean the pub. It's Friday, remember?"

Without the structure of training and playing and a regular nine-to-five in its place, days of the week didn't mean much to me anymore. Sam was my compass. "I'll be there."

"Sure? You don't have to, you know."

It was my turn to roll my eyes. "Where else would I go?"

"Nice. So you hang out with me because you have nothing better to do?"

Again, the echo of a teasing conversation we had over and over played on a loop in my head, but my usual reply escaped me. Breakfast forgotten, I slid off my stool and gripped his shoulders. "I love hanging out with you, even when you're too busy to stop by my table and call me a wanker."

Sam's wary gaze brightened with laughter. "I've never called you a wanker."

"We've got the rest of our lives. There's still time."

"BFFs, huh?"

"For real."

I let him go and he stepped away, but something unsaid hung between us. Was it so hard for him to admit he didn't want to leave and for me to beg him to stay? To blow off school and work and spend the day with me in the bubble of hard-won monotony I'd built around myself?

Apparently so. Sam flashed me a slow, sweet smile, and then he left. And I ate my solitary breakfast with growing unease at how our normal had become so complicated.

I left for the gym with a heavy heart. Out on the street, the weather suited my mood: grey and damp, but with pockets of sunshine that made no sense. And that was my city all over. London had the unique ability to feel like home and the end of the world, all wrapped up in a bow dipped in poison. Dramatic, but my brain was leaning that way these days, and not in the fashion I was used to.

I was so fucking torn up over Sam. I'd literally never felt as confused about something, even when I'd first realised my obsession with Ryan Giggs had jack all to do with his ball skills. On the one hand, I'd meant every argument I'd made for protecting our friendship. On the other, kissing Sam had been so mind-blowing, I couldn't contemplate living the rest of my life without ever doing it again.

Which is why you're an idiot for doing it in the first place.

Fair, but he'd kissed me first, a fact I clung to late at night when I was alone in bed *a fucking week* since those magical ten minutes we'd spent on the seafront. I barely remembered limping back to his parents' house after . . . or eating two plates of his ma's roast pork and crackling, and the train ride home the following day had been a blur of dread and excitement that was still my constant companion. But I remembered every millisecond our lips had been fused together, every brush of skin and snatched breath. I just wished I knew what the hell to do with it. And with Sam living his best life as though nothing had changed, I did the most ridiculous thing I could think of and confided in Freddie over a lunchtime workout.

He had his back to me as I rambled my life story from the last few weeks, sparring with the punch bag. I half expected him to laugh, but when he was done, he spun to face me with an expression I couldn't decipher.

"So . . . ," he said slowly. "What you're saying is that you finally realised the two of you are mad-hot for each other, hooked up, then five minutes later, decided to stay as roommates who moon over each other forever?"

That he hadn't blinked at me throwing my queer angst in his face was one thing. That he'd totally misunderstood me was another. "Okay, number one, we didn't hook up, not even close. And two, we don't moon over each other. The fuck does that even mean?"

Freddie wiped sweat from his face and eyeballed me over his towel. "You've been surgically attached to him since you moved into his place. If you're not talking about him, you're with him. And I've told you a thousand times how he looks at you."

I scowled. "And I've told you a thousand times that you're a prick."

"So you don't want to discuss how *you* gaze at him the moment his back's turned? How you're a world away if he's anywhere nearby?"

"Fuck off."

Freddie snorted. "I thought you wanted my advice?"

It was more that I needed to speak aloud some of the thoughts rioting in my brain before I lost my fucking mind, and I couldn't get a therapist appointment until after the weekend. Not that I needed Freddie's opinion or confirmation that I'd had it bad for Sam since I'd met him. That shit was about as far from brand new as Sam's grandparents' flowerpots. "I don't know what to do."

I sounded pathetic, even to my own ears. Freddie's expression softened. He glanced around, then dropped down beside me and draped an arm around my shoulders. "What would you have done if this had happened two years ago?"

"Two years ago? You mean when I was in the closet and getting my kicks from coke-fuelled hook-ups?"

"And whatever else you were up to on Grindr or whatever. What if you'd met Sam then? What would you have done?"

"I'd never have met Sam then. He doesn't do shit like that."

"And you think that makes him too good for you? Jesus, mate. I read the other day that eighty per cent of gay men use hook-up apps, even when they're in relationships."

"Did you read a queer dude's BFF manual or something?"

"Nope. I'm just informed. And just as well, as according to you, the BFF position is, er, filled."

I sighed. "I'm not Sam's best friend."

"Why not? That's what he said, isn't it?"

Sam had said a lot of things over the last few weeks, and anti-depressants made me shit at remembering every little detail. All I knew was that we'd effectively friend-zoned each other without a reason good enough for me to explain to Freddie. "I wish it hadn't happened."

"Which bit?"

"Any of it. We were fine until things got weird. I want things to go back to the way they were before."

"Ain't gonna happen, mate. It was always going to get complicated between you two eventually."

"Oh, really?" I tried to keep the sarcasm out of my voice. Failed.

Freddie didn't give a shit. "Really," he said. "Look, I thought it was weird when you moved in with a stranger and didn't get your own place, but it made sense after a while when I saw how calm you were around him. It was like everything that had been bothering you all these years went away."

"That was the pills the quacks gave me."

"No, it was Sam. It was being around a gay dude without having to pretend you were someone else, and living like a normal human being. Then you got closer. And by now, well, face it, dude, the only thing you *don't* do together is fuck."

I tried to unpick Freddie's theory. To find the mistruths and plot holes, but there were none, because he was right. The only thing he hadn't thought of was the ugly phenomenon that had fucked me up in the first place. "We can't be together," I whispered. "The paps, the media . . . they'll ruin his life. It's a miracle they haven't already."

"You don't think he's prepared for that? I know he's not a football fan, but he knew who you were before you moved in. That if the paps figured out he was queer, he'd be in for it too. Sam's not stupid, mate."

Of course he wasn't. Even using the word in the same sentence as his name made me want to chin Freddie.

He knew it, too. He got up and jerked his head towards the changing rooms. "Come on," he said. "Let's get some lunch."

11

Sam

Micah never came to the pub at lunchtime, so it was fair to say I was pretty surprised when he rocked up with Freddie just after midday. And embarrassed, as I hadn't seen Freddie since I'd petulantly ignored his message. A message that, if I'd taken it the way he'd meant it, could've saved me and Micah weeks of awkward bullshit.

Luckily for me, Freddie seemed to have forgotten all about it and treated me with the same mild amusement he always did, leaving me to ignore him.

Business as usual. At least it would've been if Micah's gaze wasn't drilling holes in me. *Why is he here?* Cos I knew it wasn't for the Noble Fox's average club sandwiches.

"Do you want me to take over their table?" Céleste stage whispered.

"Why would I want that?"

"Because you look like a rabbit in headlights."

"Do not." To strengthen my argument, I picked up the tray with Micah and Freddie's drinks and carried it to the booth where they'd set up shop. Micah seemed to track my every move, but he didn't speak. Only Freddie murmured a quiet thanks.

Disturbed, I retreated to where Céleste was watching the whole thing play out with her hands on her hips. "Something's changed," she said.

"Hmm?"

"Between you two. Did something happen?"

"Nope. We're fine." I'd always been a shit liar, and I'd done enough of it the last few weeks to last me a lifetime. *"Then we carry on as we are. Nothing ever has to change. We're all right, aren't we?"* Flushing, I turned away from Céleste and made a meal of topping-up-gin garnishes that were already fully stocked.

She snorted and moved off, but her painfully accurate observation stayed with me. Jesus. Was I that transparent? Could strangers tell that I was crazy about my roommate?

"Sam?"

I jumped. Micah was leaning over the bar, peering at me crouched down by the fridge. His dark eyes were brimming with anxiety. Alarmed, I scrambled to my feet and forced a smile. "What's up?"

His frown remained. "I need to talk to you."

"Now? Micah, I'm working."

"I know. I meant later. Are you doing anything after work?"

The sum total of my plans had been to sink a few gins, then meander home in the hope that the mess I'd made of our friendship would've magically fixed itself. "I'm not doing anything. I'll be home around seven."

Micah nodded slowly. "Can we talk then?"

"What about?"

"About everything. This shit is driving me crazy."

We'd talked already, round and round and round and round. I couldn't see what he could possibly say that would bring anything new to the table. He'd made his feelings perfectly clear: he liked kissing me and he'd always wanted to, but he disliked himself too much to let us just . . . *be*. And I got it, I really did, but I didn't like it, and hiding my unjustified resentment was exhausting.

Still, refusing him anything when he was looking at me the way he was right then was a task for a man far stronger than me. "Whatever you want. Just feed me, okay? I can't do deep and meaningful on an empty stomach."

For a moment, his gaze flared with mirth, like a dirty joke had flitted into his convoluted mind. Then the shutters came down again and he nodded. "I can do that."

He returned to his table. Him and Freddie shared a plate of chicken salad with a side of chips, then they left without saying goodbye, leaving me to the mercy of Céleste's twitching eyebrows and the six hours left on my shift.

Time passed like it was rooted in treacle. I began to miss the cigarettes I'd given up five years ago and seriously contemplated raiding Céleste's. But the thought of returning home with the stench clinging to my skin and clothes stopped me. Just. Settling for checking my phone every ten minutes wasn't any less ridiculous.

I left a Sam-shaped hole in the door when my shift finally ended, but outside, doubt and nerves hit home. Micah had never asked me for a serious conversation—when they happened, it was by accident. What if he wanted to move out? To run from the clusterfuck I'd created? The prospect of living without him made me sick to my stomach, but . . . maybe it was for the best. For *him*. I'd tried and tried to go back to normal and keep our home the sanctuary it had once been for him, but man, acting chill around a man whose kiss had set me on fire was *hard*, in more ways than one. Something had to give, and perhaps Micah had decided it would be him.

It took me three minutes to get home. Despite my trepidation, agitation won out and I speed-walked the whole way to the front door.

I let myself in, bracing myself for silence—*what if he already left?* —but soft music greeted me and the scent of something so delicious I had to double-check I'd waltzed into the right flat.

Somehow, I had.

I ditched my coat and shoes and followed the smell to the kitchen. Micah was slumped over the counter, chest to the cheap laminate as he poked at his phone. He glanced up as I laid eyes on my nan's cast iron pot simmering on the stove and the dish of garlic-flecked rice already prepared. "Did you have a lobotomy?"

"You're not that lucky, but I figured you'd be hungry."

"I'm always hungry. You've never cooked for me before."

"I haven't done a lot of things."

The sentence was so loaded it almost distracted me from whatever was in the pot. Almost. Nothing was going to stop me lifting the lid and peeking inside. "What's this?"

"*Feijoada.* My mum used to cook it every Sunday."

"She doesn't anymore?"

"I wouldn't know."

His tone was flat, devoid of bitterness and pain, but I knew better. I set the pan lid aside and stirred the dark mix of meat and beans around. "Whatever it is, it smells amazing. When can we eat it?"

"Um . . . now? It finished cooking a while ago. I've just been keeping it warm."

Sitting down to a meal Micah had cooked was ten shades of surreal, but the awkwardness of it faded as soon as the smoky, meaty stew he served up hit my tongue. It tasted a thousand times better than it smelt, and the rice was unbelievable. I half cleared my plate before I found coherent words. "This is incredible. How am I only just now finding out you can cook?"

"Because it's not true. I can make one thing, and that's only because it involved putting meat and beans in a pot and falling asleep."

"Yeah, well. Feel free to do it more often." I ate more food while Micah pushed his around his plate. As my greed was sated, the anxiety that had carried me home returned. *Fuck. Maybe he really is going to move out.*

The mountain of delicious food he'd cooked me turned to stone in my gut. I shoved my plate away and reached for the beer he'd put in front of me. “Let’s have it then,” I said. “What do you want to talk about?”

Micah picked up our plates and carried them to the sink. He turned the tap on, rinsed them, and stacked them in the dishwasher before he faced me again. “I want to take back what I said the other day.”

“Which part?”

“I don’t know, I can’t remember it all. Whichever part made you think I don’t want you.”

“You never said you didn’t want me. Just that you weren’t . . . well enough, I guess, to explore how you feel.”

Micah sighed. “That’s still true, but I’m having a really hard time accepting it.”

Every nerve in my body screamed at me to get up and go to him. To put my arms around him and smooth the worry lines from his face, but caution countered instinct. I took a deep breath. “What do you mean?”

“I mean that I don’t want to ignore what happened, and I don’t want you to feel as though you have to. For a while, I wished it hadn’t happened at all, but I don’t want that either.”

“What *do* you want, Micah?”

He took a step forward. Stopped. Took another step. “I don’t . . . fuck, I don’t know. But I can’t live like this. I can’t live with you feeling like you did something wrong when you putting your lips on me like that was all I’ve ever wanted.”

My heart stuttered to a painful halt and restarted with a savage kick to my ribcage. “I don’t feel like what we did was wrong, but I respect that it’s not what you want right now.”

“But it is!” Micah shouted. “Don’t you get it? I *do* want it. I want *you*. I always have.”

I flinched. Couldn’t help it. I was a feisty mofo in my own right, but it had been a long time since a dude had last yelled at me. And it was the first time I’d ever heard Micah raise his voice. I stood and went to him. I put my hands on his chest. His heart thudded wildly against my palm and his arms trembled. "It's okay to want me and do nothing about it. I'm your friend. You don't owe me anything."

"I don't want to just be your friend. I want more."

He spoke so softly I had to wonder if my own thoughts had betrayed me. If I'd unconsciously spoken them aloud. But Micah's eyes said more than his words ever could. Molten with desire and fear, they entranced me, drawing me in until our faces were inches apart. "I want more too," I whispered. "But not if it's going to derail you. You've worked so hard to get better."

"As if you could ever make me worse. Dude, it's *me* that's freaking me out. Not you."

"How do we stop that, though?"

Micah shrugged, and helplessness cast a shadow over his face. "I don't know. But . . . I want to try. And I have the tools I need for that. Will you, um, be patient with me?"

I could be patient about anything except waiting another second to kiss him again. With his heart still kicking the shit out of my palm, I closed the distance between us and melted against him, fusing our lips together.

Micah staggered back against the counter, taking me with him. He seized my face in his hands and responded, and as his velvet tongue slid into my mouth, stars aligned. This was different to any kiss we'd shared before. There was no surprise, no shock and awe, just the warmth of a desire gone unspoken for far too long.

Somehow, we ended up in the hallway. My bedroom door was closest, but it was shut. Micah's door was open. He broke our kiss and took my hand. "Come with me."

12

Micah

Morning came with bright sunshine. After weeks of dull grey skies, it was like I'd opened my eyes to another world—a world where Sam lay asleep next to me, his slender arms wrapped around me, his head on my chest.

My fingers were tangled in his hair. I left them there as I came awake and took stock of the fact that he was really in my bed and what I was seeing wasn't the remnants of a fucked-up dream. It had been years since I'd slept with anyone, in the literal sense. Before Sam, spending the night with someone had involved a pocketful of coke and faceless sex. With him, we'd kissed for hours and then fallen asleep in our clothes, and I wouldn't change a fucking thing.

Except maybe that my leg was so stiff and sore it felt like my nerves had been replaced with jagged glass. And the fact that I had to get up and neck my medication before I got jittery, which meant disturbing Sam and leaving the nest we'd built around us in my bed.

Fuck my life.

As if he'd heard my inner bitch, Sam stirred. He slid off me and stretched before he seemed to realise where he was.

I sat up on my elbows to watch him blink like a cartoon version of himself. His eyes widened as his gaze fell on me, and a laugh bubbled out of me, surprising both of us. I legit couldn't remember the last time I'd laughed before lunchtime.

Sam scrunched his beautiful face and swatted me with a pillow. "What are you grinning at?"

"You."

"Why?"

"Cos you're funny."

"It's not my usual vibe."

"Oh, I know. We live together, remember? I know exactly how unfunny you are."

Sam moved like a goddamn ninja and replaced the pillow he'd tossed on my chest. He straddled me, arms braced on either side of my head, and dropped his face down low enough that I could've picked up where we left off last night if I'd had the balls. *And why don't you? It's not like you didn't kiss a thousand times last night.*

I had no answer to that. All I knew was that if Sam was going to sit on top of me like this for a prolonged length of time, then we were never leaving this room.

Ever.

Like he'd read my mind, Sam sat back and circled his hips with just enough pressure to let me know I wasn't imagining it. My body responded like a fucking firework. Heat rushed me, and my dick was an instant stone column.

I groaned and closed my eyes. "If you're gonna do that, you'd better follow through."

"With what? Is there something you want?"

I couldn't look at him. He'd warned me before shit got complicated between us that he had a filthy mouth, but self-preservation had allowed me to forget. And there was no way I was verbalising what I wanted to do with him. Dirty talk or no, I didn't want to scare him. Or myself. Man, when did sex get so complicated?

When you stopped fucking randos and fell in love with your roommate.

Love.

Jesus.

I opened my eyes. Sam was watching me with a speculative gaze. He was still on top of me, still grinding, slow and sweet, lip caught in his teeth. I slid my hands beneath his T-shirt. His skin was so fucking smooth and warm. I needed to feel him against me.

Smirking, he hooked it over his head and tossed it aside. I reached for him, and—

My phone rang.

"Fuck's sake." I fumbled for it and peered at the screen. Freddie's face grinned back at me, and I cursed the day I'd ever met him, let alone given him my number.

Sam bent down and brushed his lips over my ear. "Answer it."

"No."

"Yes. I need coffee anyway."

There was nothing I needed more than him, but I let him go. *Fool.*

He hopped out of bed and slipped out of the room, leaving me to miss Freddie's call and shuffle to my chest of drawers to down my faithful handful of pills. A message from Freddie flashed up on my phone screen.

Freddie: *just checking in mate. u good?*

Micah: *why wouldn't I be?*

Freddie: *a simple yes would do*

Micah: *yes*

Freddie: :) :) :)

I scowled at the smiley faces. I didn't share Sam's obsession with proper words and full sentences, but emojis got on my tits. What was Freddie sending me a bright yellow grin supposed to mean? That me being an ungrateful arsehole made him happy?

"What are you glaring at?"

"Hmm?"

Sam came up behind me. He put his hands on my hips, and I ached for him to slide his arms around me. "You're glowering at your phone like you want to toss it out the window."

"Oh." I made an effort to soften my expression. It didn't help that I'd been born with a resting bitch face, but being around Sam usually blunted my sharp edges. "Sorry. Just Freddie being annoying."

"How so?"

"He's a nosy fucker."

"What does he want to know?"

"If I'm okay."

"Are you?"

"Yes."

Sam said nothing, but his presence behind me seemed to shout something I couldn't decipher. I turned to face him. His focus wasn't on me, it was zeroed in on the pill packet still clutched in my hand.

I shoved it back in the drawer. "Sorry."

Sam's eyebrows hit his hairline. "What on earth for?"

"Um. Dunno?"

"Did you think I was going to pill shame you or some other messed up bullshit? Because if you did, you don't know me at all, and we have serious problems as roommates, let alone anything else."

The anything else tacked on the end of that sentence made my head spin, but for once it was in the right direction. "I didn't think that. I'm just . . . I don't know. Embarrassed, maybe?"

"Of what? Anti-depressants? Come on, man." Like magic, the complications of the last however long it had been, faded away. Sam stood in front of me as the rock of a friend he'd always been and shook his head. "I kind of guessed you were on medication alongside your therapy appointments, especially when you told me you needed pills to get out of bed in the morning. It's not a thing, Micah. Do you really think I'm that kind of wanker?"

"I don't think you're a wanker at all."

"Sure about that?"

"Fuck yeah." Unless he meant something dirty. I could dig that. *Focus.* My hands shook. I clenched my fists, but the temptation to touch him was too strong to resist. I pulled him closer, pressing our bodies together. "I didn't hide it on purpose."

"I know."

"I really liked sharing my bed with you."

"I know that too."

"How?"

Sam *finally* wrapped his arms around me, grounding me with an embrace that was familiar, safe, and yet brand-fucking new. "You were carving a hole in my back all night long."

"Oh. Sorry."

"Don't be. I liked it." He cupped my cheek in his heated palm and drew my face down to his. "I liked everything about it and . . . waking up with you."

He kissed me and my brain fell silent. Primal desire overcame me, and I was on him before I truly knew what I was doing.

I lifted him clean off his feet and walked him back to my bed, ignoring the wrench in my gnarled up leg. We fell onto the mess we'd left behind, and I fought with the jeans he'd somehow slept in. My sweats and Nike tee were more accommodating. They landed somewhere beyond the bed; I didn't care where. How could I when Sam was naked on my bed, and I was naked too, writhing on top of him, grinding, desperate for friction?

An evil voice lived in my head. It had been there since I'd first got a boner for Ryan Giggs, telling me every moment I was with a bloke that it would ruin me and cement my status as a reliable disappointment to my parents. In the end, my constant fuck-ups had given it the validation it craved, but health and healing had kept it at bay since I'd met Sam, and as I rolled onto my back and pulled him on top of me, its warning call didn't sound. For the first time in my life, I was stronger.

Sam rose up on his knees. My dick dug into his back, hard and insistent, but I was transfixed by his. It was as if I'd never seen one before, and I *ached* for it. I ached for *him*.

Perhaps sensing my desperation, Sam tilted his head sideways. "What do you want?"

"I want you in my mouth." The words fell out of me, but I meant every syllable. I needed him in my mouth before I legit combusted. Needed him to slide down my throat and fill my senses. "Please?"

The tension in Sam's shoulders melted away, his questioning

frown replaced by a smirk that sent shivers down my spine. He walked forward on his knees, straddling my chest, and brought his cock to my lips, demanding entrance.

I let him in and swallowed him whole, moaning as his ragged groan shattered the heated quiet. My hands found their way to his thighs as though I'd gripped the sinewy muscle a thousand times, and I drew him forwards, hoping he'd decipher the message: *fuck my mouth.*

"Yeah?" Sam whispered. "You want it?"

I wanted it like I'd never wanted anything. I opened my throat and gripped him harder. He cried out and grabbed the headboard for support and thrust into my mouth, slowly at first, but then with more force as I urged him on. He was so hard. My jaw ached as I worked him, and I couldn't get enough of the salty fluid leaking onto my tongue. The old me had approached my sexuality like a fucking dictator, taking what I thought I wanted and giving little in return, but this was so much better. Giving Sam pleasure lit a fire in me I knew would burn forever, and if these were my last moments on earth, I'd take them every time over anything that had come before.

Desire careened through me like a wrecking ball. I dug my fingers into Sam's soft flesh, breathed deep through my nose, losing myself to his scent. It wasn't long before he growled out my name and shot in my mouth, and I mourned the thrill of it as his shudders eased and faded away. I wanted to do this forever. Every day, every night, every moment he'd let me.

Jesus. If I'd been upright, I might've stumbled. I clung to Sam's thighs as he turned my face to his with a wink. He reached for my aching dick, and realisation hit me like a fucking asteroid.

This was a seismic shift, and there was no going back.

13

Sam

The world had changed. It wasn't tangible enough for me to say how, but it had. Perhaps it was the arrival of spring. The days were longer and the skies brighter. The dark of the winter was gone, and maybe my black mood had gone with it.

Or, maybe the lift in my spirits had something to do with Micah swallowing my dick at every opportunity he got, and the fact that he seemed delighted with himself for doing it. He was so enthusiastic he often put me into an orgasm coma before I could reciprocate, but that was something I was working on.

"That's your third Red Bull." Céleste plucked the can from my hand and tossed it, half-full, into the bin. "You'll give yourself a heart attack."

I didn't have the stones to tell her that if I'd survived a dozen Micah blowjobs, I could handle an extra dose of caffeine, which was odd in itself, because I told her most things, whether she wanted to know them or not. I settled for a scowl and ate more of the chips I'd pinched from the kitchen for my lunch while scrolling through the message thread I shared with Micah. It had become more active in the past week, and though our conversations still centred around buying milk and putting the bins out, subtle clues gave away the shift in our friendship: my sudden interest in his PT schedule, and his daily enquiry as to when I'd be home. Weaker moments had me wondering if he was bored now the weather was better and he was still spending much of his time home alone. Then I'd remember the fire in his gaze every time he touched me, and everything made sense.

My chips ran out. With a heavy sigh, I took my bowl to the kitchen and returned to the bar. It was Wednesday, and the pub was busy with city wankers treating themselves to a hump-day liquid lunch. They were messy bastards, far worse than the working-class boozers I'd served up north. When I wasn't collecting glasses, I was sweeping up scattered food and gathering discarded newspapers. Most were the poncy broadsheets the yuppie types liked to carry under one arm to look clever, folded and unread. A few were the tabloids they really liked.

I rescued a copy of *The Sun* and spared it an absent glance. My teenage years were littered with memories of me studying the women on page three and trying to figure out why their cheeky smiles and great boobs did nothing for me, but as an adult, the sensationalist headlines did my head in. That, and the harassment of people like Micah just trying to live their lives. Case-in-point, the papped photo of him and Freddie in the gym, along with a stellar caption: *Gay Footballer Micah Phillips Cosies Up To Freddie Santos!*

Jesus wept. He's not even gay. Is it so hard to spell bisexual? Disgusted, I flounced out of the pub and dumped the rag in a street bin, resisting the urge to set it on fire. It wasn't the first time Micah had been caught unawares at work, but I'd never seen him so affectionate with Freddie, leaning into him while Freddie had his arm draped around his shoulders. I knew there was nothing in it, but god, it *burned* that Micah was doing that with Freddie in public and not me.

He doesn't suck Freddie's dick, though, does he? And he hugs you all the time. Always has.

Not by choice, though. At least, not in the beginning. I recalled with perfect clarity the first time I'd hugged Micah goodnight. He'd been so adorably surprised I'd done it again and again until it had become an almost regular thing. Until recently, he'd never initiated it, but over time, his response had grown so warm I'd been addicted. Was still addicted, to that and everything else about him.

"What are you scowling about?"

Startled, I whirled around to face the last person on earth I wanted to see.

Freddie Santos smirked back at me. "Take it you've seen the paper?"

"Uh-huh. Just now. Has Micah seen it?"

Freddie shrugged. "No idea. Don't worry about it, though. There's worse things in the world than being linked to my fine self."

I eyed him warily. "What about you? Aren't you worried what it'll do to your rep?"

"Not really. I'm privileged enough that I don't have to. They can take all the pictures of me they want. I have nothing to hide."

Of course he didn't. Freddie Santos was as uber heterosexual as they came, and I irrationally hated him for it, despite the knowledge that if Micah had been just like him, I wouldn't be counting the minutes until I could run home and rip his clothes off.

Freddie took my silence for doubt. He nudged me. "Seriously, dude. Don't worry about it. At least if they think I'm banging him, they'll stay off your tail for a while."

"My tail?"

"Yeah. You and Micah can't keep it indoors forever."

I blinked. For reasons I didn't quite understand, it hadn't occurred to me that Micah had told Freddie—or anyone else—about us. I'd accepted the fact that keeping it "indoors" was a forever status and hadn't considered the consequences of doing otherwise. I cast an uneasy glance at the bin. Micah's low profile meant that he bored the paparazzi enough for their attention to be sporadic. Would that change if he had a boyfriend?

As if he even wants you to be his boyfriend, fool. Does friends with benefits mean nothing to you?

I really was a fool. Not because I was pondering my boyfriend status in the middle of the street while Freddie looked on, but because it didn't matter. I'd promised Micah over and over that I was his friend, and that came before anything. Before photos of him in the newspapers with other men, and before my pathetic desire to put a label on whatever was brewing between us. *Stop angsting.*

Easier said than done, but as Freddie said his goodbyes and meandered away, home time couldn't come soon enough.

Micah was exactly where I expected him to be, slouched on the couch in front of midweek football, pretending he wasn't utterly obsessed. Much had changed in recent weeks, but not that.

I shut the door with a quiet click and took the pizza I'd picked up on my way home to the coffee table.

A copy of *The Sun* greeted me, opened to the Freddie snap. "So you saw it, huh?"

Micah slid me a slow stare from behind his hood. "My ex-agent gave me a heads up. Though, actually, he was never my agent for real. He quit before we signed the contract."

"But you're still in touch?"

"No. He's just a good guy with stuff like this."

I opened one of the beer bottles I'd slid in my pocket on my way out of the pub. "Can't be that good if he quit on you."

"He didn't quit on *me*." Micah waved the beer away. "He left the game to build houses with Dom."

"Ramos?"

"Yup. They're BFFs. Oh, and Isha's queer as fuck too, which I didn't know till about a month ago. I thought he was married with kids and shit."

"You can do all those things and still be bi or pan. Don't erase yourself."

Micah snorted. "And don't you be lecturing me. I know what I am."

"Sorry. You know I can't help being a smart arse."

"I like your arse."

"Good to know." I picked up the newspaper to cover my blush. Getting used to Micah being casually sexual with me—or at all—was very much still a thing. "I saw Freddie today. He didn't seem bothered about being labelled your boyfriend."

"Where did you see Freddie?"

"Outside the pub. I thought he might be coming to see you."

"He didn't."

"Oh. Maybe he was going to the gym then."

"Doubt it. He's playing tonight." Micah jerked his head at the TV screen, but all I saw were blobs of coloured shirts kicking a lump of white leather. I had zero clue who was playing and even less interest in finding out.

I opened the pizza box and helped myself to a wedge of the garlic prawn pizza Micah adored. Laced with chilli and herbs, it was about as sexy as cheese-covered bread could get, and fuck, it was good. I demolished my slice in two seconds flat and looked up, expecting to find Micah laughing at me, but his stare was troubled.

Appetite postponed, I turned away from the pizza. "What's the matter?"

"Nothing."

"Liar."

"Am I?"

"Yup. Normal service would have you fighting me for this pizza."

"I wouldn't win."

"But you'd try."

He glanced at the pizza box and shook his head. "It shouldn't be this complicated."

"What shouldn't?"

"*This.*" Micah got up and limped around the back of the couch. "We shouldn't be hiding indoors with a pizza box with bullshit photos like that as an audience."

"Um . . . we're not hiding, bro. I've spent all day in the pub with an audience. Even if you weren't here, I'd still be kicking it on the couch and stuffing my face."

Micah smirked, but it was brief. He folded his arms across his chest. "Don't pretend you don't know what I mean."

"I'm not. I was angsting about the same nonsense after I saw Freddie. How it was okay for you to get papped with him because it wasn't real, but if they caught you with me, they'd figure out there was more to it."

"I can't let them catch us."

"What? Never? That's not realistic. Even if we weren't doing anything, we live together. It's a miracle it's not happened before now."

"It hasn't happened because we never go anywhere together. We get all our shopping delivered, and even at the pub, I come and go without you."

"We go to the library."

"Once. And I doubt paps would ever come looking for me there. I'm not exactly known for my intelligence."

I rolled my eyes, already over this conversation. "That's because no one knows you at all, apart from the football and the orgies."

Micah sighed. "I've told you a thousand times there were no orgies."

"You've told me once."

"So? Don't you see that's the point? That I wish you didn't need to know?"

"Which part?"

"All of it. I wish we were strangers."

My appetite evaporated for good, taking with it the buzz I'd carried all day at the prospect of spending the evening with him. "Awesome. So you wish you'd never met me? Thanks for that, mate."

I took my beer and stood. Micah made a grab for me, but I evaded and left the room, retreating to the cool dark of my bedroom. I shut the door with more force than necessary, pretty safe in the assumption that he wouldn't follow me.

Or so I thought. My bedroom door opened. Micah leaned against the frame. "I didn't mean it like that."

"I know."

"Why are you so pissed then?"

"Because I wish we were strangers too. I wish we'd met in a bar and you didn't hate yourself so much you'd rather not know me at all than deal with the fact that everything I really know about you has come from the fucking media."

"What?"

I emptied my pockets onto my chest of drawers with shaky hands: keys, phone, wallet. I usually did it in the hallway, but my eagerness to get to Micah had been so absolute, I'd forgotten. Now, I did it to buy myself time before everything hurt, but the task was over far too soon. I dropped my keys and turned to face Micah in the darkness. "You won't let me in."

Micah shifted. "The fuck does that mean?"

"It means if you weren't a footballer who'd had his life splashed all over the internet, I wouldn't know anything about you, and half of that probably isn't true."

"That's not fair."

"Isn't it? Tell me something you've shared with me, something I haven't dragged out of you kicking and screaming or guessed close enough to the truth that you've told me the rest?"

Micah flinched as my words seemed to hit him one by one, chipping away at his armour but not getting through. I hated him for being so vulnerable and yet so unreachable, and I hated myself even more.

"Fuck." I knocked my fists against my temples. "This is coming out all wrong, but can't you see what I'm saying just a little bit?"

"I don't even know what you're trying to say," he said flatly. "Apart from the fact that I've been disappointing you all along. What do you *want*, Sam? My life story written on the front door so you see it first?"

"What? No! I want *you* to tell me so I don't have to make assumptions or rely on bullshit rumours. Micah, I don't even know what happened to you on that fucking train platform. Do you know how that feels? To not know if you really did jump?"

"Jump?"

"Yeah. Jump. Cos that's what it said on the internet. That you threw yourself in front of an incoming train—"

Nausea cut me off. That and shock that our encounter had taken such a catastrophic nosedive. Jesus. I'd come home for a pizza and a cuddle, not to attack festering wounds with a pickaxe. *What the hell are you doing?* But the dam had broken. It wasn't enough that Micah had admitted that he felt anywhere near how I felt about him. It wasn't enough that he made my body sing with his devilish mouth. And it never would be as long as I couldn't make him understand how much I needed to *know* him. "Look, I'm sorry, okay? I just—I can't live with my own version of events. It tortures me."

"Why?"

"You know why! Because I fucking love you."

My shout pierced the air and seemed to rattle around the room like a curse. The shock in my bones morphed into dread and I slapped my hand over my mouth as if I could press every word I'd uttered in the last ten minutes back in. I'd told Micah not to erase himself, but fuck, I wanted to disappear.

The feeling increased with every second that Micah stared at me with his dead gaze. *He doesn't believe me.* More than that, he didn't want to because accepting love meant everything he believed about himself was wrong, and that maybe, just maybe, giving up on himself was impossible.

I let my hand drop. "Micah, come here. Please?"

He didn't move. For a long moment, neither did I, but the need to be close to him overrode my fear of rejection. I kicked off my shoes and padded across the carpet. Micah was a statue of tension—shoulders, neck, jaw. I wondered if he'd even heard what I'd said or if he was stuck on me demanding he tell me every detail of the worst moments of his life. Shame crept over me. I fought his locked arms and pulled him close, burying my head in his chest. "I'm sorry, okay? I'm so sorry. I just get so frustrated that you don't let me—or anyone else—love you the way you deserve."

"I don't want anyone else to love me."

It felt like forever since he'd spared me a full sentence. I blinked up at him. *What does that mean?* But the question stuck in my throat. Speaking without thought had led us into this unholy mess in the first place.

Life crept into Micah's eyes. Aggravation first, then panic as whatever he was searching for in my face couldn't be found. He sucked in a breath and gripped my shoulders so hard a pained grunt escaped me. "I mean it, Sam. I don't want anyone else to love me. Only you. It's only ever been you. I just wish— *Fuck.*" He squeezed his eyes shut and shook his head. "I just wish I knew what was me."

I eased his hands from my shoulders and twined his fingers with mine. "What do you mean?"

"I don't know."

"Yes, you do. Tell me."

Micah opened his eyes, his expression brimming with despair. "I don't know how I feel about anything. I never have. Before I got outed, I didn't feel anything, like, ever. I was dead inside. The only time I felt alive was when I was playing, snorting coke, or paying Grindr hook-ups to keep quiet. And it was like that for bare years, man, so I just kept playing and sniffing and fucking, hoping it would kill me in the end."

"How does a professional athlete have a coke habit?"

He shrugged. "It's all in the timing and who you know. For a while there, I was a connected motherfucker."

I could believe it. I *did* believe it. "Keep talking."

"Can we sit on your bed?"

"Of course."

I led him across the room. Micah limped behind me, his leg dragging more than usual, but I held my tongue and motioned for him to sit.

He obeyed, still holding my hands in a death grip, and I remembered the long trip north, rocking along with the train while he held onto me for dear life.

I pried one hand free and thumbed the worry lines on his face. "Talk, Micah. Please?"

"I'm trying."

"I know."

Micah sighed. Again. "They said the anti-depressants and mood stabilisers would make me feel like a zombie for a while. I never told them I already did. But . . . it didn't work out like that. I started taking them a few weeks before we met, and everything's been different since then. It scares me."

"Why?"

"Cos I don't know what's real. What's me and what's the magic pills. I won't be on them forever, and then what? What if my brain shuts down again and I forget that I love you too?"

He loves me. His other words sunk in, but those precious three hovered at the surface. "You love me?"

Micah's troubled frown turned incredulous. "Of course I do. I always have. How can you not know that?"

"Because you've never told me. I'm not a mind reader." I spoke with a smile, but inside, I was reeling. Micah loved me. All this time and I'd had no idea, even when he'd confessed that he wanted to kiss me. That he'd wanted to kiss me for a long time.

Micah flopped back on my bed, taking me with him. "I'm such a dick."

"Not in a bad way."

"Huh?"

I found a grin and stroked his face again: the smudges under his eyes, his sculpted cheekbones, and strong jaw. "I like your dick."

"Very funny."

"I try."

Humour flared in his dark eyes, but it was gone in a flash. He rolled onto his side to face me. "I want to love you. You know that, don't you?"

I didn't. How could I when so much of this conversation had said the opposite? But I couldn't bear his raw panic. It struck my heart with its blunt blade and I needed it gone. "Let's think about it logically," I said. "Anti-depressants take months to start working. You said everything changed when we met, which was only a few weeks after you started taking them. What did you mean?"

A shy smile threatened Micah's frown. "Aw, don't make me say it."

I sat up and loomed over him. "I have to. It's the law."

"Says who?"

"Says me. You can't tell me you love me and not fill in the blanks."

"It was the way you looked at me."

"How so?"

Micah shrugged. "Like you'd never seen me before. I mean, I knew the moment you realised you had, but it didn't matter cos you didn't change, and I loved you for that from the start."

He'd once told me that confronting his emotions, for better or worse, exhausted him. And I'd seen him after therapy sessions often enough to know that he was done talking. There was no more, at least, not today.

His eyes grew heavy, and I knew if I didn't move him, he'd fall asleep right where he lay. "Come on." I nudged him. "Take your clothes off."

"Huh?" Of course he was suddenly alert.

"Not like that . . . unless you want to. I meant, don't sleep in your clothes."

His gaze was unreadable. He sat up and tugged his T-shirt over his head. His ripped torso was everything, and heat bloomed in every part of me. I wished with all my heart, just for a moment, that he was easy. That I could lunge at him and spend the rest of the night exploring him without caution and complication, but nothing about Micah was easy, for him or for me.

I coaxed him into my bed and got him to curl on his side with his head on my chest. My hands found their way to his hair, and I let my fingers rub absently over his scalp as I considered the fact that he still hadn't told me what had happened to him in that damn-fucking tube station.

Like he'd read my mind, he sighed. "I know you're upset that I won't talk about it, but I *can't*. You understand that, don't you? It fucks me up too much. I'm . . . too close to it. My therapist made me a few months back, and I couldn't sleep for days after. It was like, fuck, I don't know. Like it happened over and over again every time I closed my eyes. It only stopped when you were around."

I could pinpoint the exact time period he was talking about. It had been right after Christmas, that weird week in between the big day and the new year. At the time, I'd figured he was missing his family and had been glad I'd come home on Boxing Day. But now it all made sickening sense—his lack of appetite, the all-night pacing, his agitation every time I left the flat, even though he'd barely spoken to me. "I'm a good distraction, eh?"

"It's not that. It's more you remind me that there's more."

I wanted to push him. To dissect every syllable until there was no doubt what he meant, but he really was done now. He dozed off while I hummed emo Mallory Knox tunes and wondered what the hell tomorrow would bring. When I was sure he was asleep, I kissed his temple and whispered to the moon, "We'll figure it out, I promise."

14

Micah

I woke alone, as I had for ninety per cent of my life, but instead of normalcy, fear gripped me, and I bolted upright with a startled gasp, heart pounding, eyes darting around a room that wasn't mine.

A full-blown panic attack threatened. Then I remembered: we'd slept in Sam's bed. And I liked it. Being surrounded by him, even though he wasn't there, slowed my racing heart.

It also helped that I remembered what day it was and why Sam wasn't here at arse o'clock in the morning. On Thursdays, he went to college for his English Lit classes and often came home with a grin on his face I dreamt about for days after. The kind of grin someone got when they'd spent the day doing the one thing they really loved.

The kind of grin I felt splitting my face in the rare moments I let myself enjoy being with him. Sometimes in the afterglow of kissing him or sucking his dick, but mostly when he laughed.

I sat up in his bed, wincing as the stiff muscles in my leg protested. It was early, but I already knew that bastard was going to give me a bad day. A hot shower would help, and Sam's en suite called my name. I rarely used it, preferring to use the ancient bathroom his grandparents never got around to refurbishing, and let him have the shower that actually worked all to himself, but on days like this, temptation got the better of me.

Grimacing, I hauled myself out of Sam's bed and into my own room to get my meds. My leg dragged behind me, heavy and useless, too stiff to move and too weak to bear weight. It hurt too, like a motherfucker, so I palmed some muscle relaxants and swallowed them down with my usual morning cocktail.

On my way back to Sam's bathroom, I spotted my phone abandoned on the coffee table. I swiped it and took it with me to cancel my afternoon clients. I could sit on the sidelines and watch other people work out any day of the week, but walking to the gym was going to be a problem. *You could get a taxi—*

Right, because cabbies were just lining up to drive people for a three-minute fare.

I rescheduled the sessions and tried—and failed—to not feel guilty about it. Disquiet gnawed in my gut. After a lifetime of letting people down, these days I couldn't swallow it. Most of my clients were like Sam: they didn't care who I was or where I'd come from, and they enjoyed my company, albeit paid for. And I liked theirs too. My job got me out of the house. Without it, I was just some loser limping around someone else's flat by myself.

Not that I did much limping around once the muscle relaxants kicked in. My limbs were jelly. I lay down on the living room floor and stared at the ceiling. I wanted Sam, but I never messaged him when he was at college, so I settled for finally answering Freddie's texts from the day before.

He called me straight back. "You're alive then."

Depends on your definition. But I didn't bother to fill him in on my current predicament. He'd seen enough of that recently. "Sorry you got caught up in my shit. Did you get any grief at the game?"

Freddie snorted. "Probably, but you know I don't listen. If some cockhead wants to call me a fag, let them. I said it to Sam, it's just words to me, man."

"Lucky you."

"I said that too, or words to that effect, but your boy wasn't feeling particularly chatty."

"He's not my—never mind. What were you doing outside the Fox anyway?"

"I was coming to see you, but I changed my mind after I saw Sam. Figured it wasn't my ugly mug you needed to lay eyes on."

Freddie was *far* from ugly, but I knew better than to tell him. I'd never hear the end of it. Besides, whatever he'd seen in Sam scared the hell out of me. I couldn't let the hangovers of my old life hurt him too. "I don't know what to do."

"Are you still stuck on that?"

"Yeah, but in a different way. Dude, I can't have paps getting in his face like they do you and me. That picture's a joke to you cos it's not real, but if that was him, it'd be his whole fucking life flayed open. I can't subject him to that."

Freddie sighed. "Valid, but you don't get to choose what he's subjected to. He's a grown man. And he's far from naïve, at least I thought he was until I saw his face yesterday. Fuck, I guess there are no right answers."

"I'm tired of being an angsty weirdo."

"Then stop."

If only it were that easy. I let Freddie go and stayed on the floor with my eyes closed, fighting every morbid thought that crossed my mind. The muscle relaxants made it easier than usual. My body melded with the carpet. The floorboards became my bones, and before long, I was sinking like that dude in *Trainspotting*.

Sam

"*Micah.* Wake *up*." I shook him, panic rearing up in my throat. Logic told me he was sleeping, but with his pale skin and slack limbs, he was scaring the hell out of me. Besides, why the fuck would he be shirtless and passed out on the living room floor?

I could think of no reasonable answer. I shook him again, worst-case scenarios having a rave in my imagination, but this time he stirred. His wide, brown eyes blinked open, and as the haze cleared, he smiled, and my world came back together. "What on earth are you doing half-naked down here?"

Micah sat up on his elbows. "Taking a nap."

"I can see that, but why?"

"Crappy leg day. I was too hot, and I couldn't get comfortable."

"Oh." The most irrational worries drained from me and I sat back on my heels. "Does your leg still hurt?"

"Yeah."

"You're admitting it in real time? Wow. It must be bad."

"Nah, I just remember what happened last time I didn't tell you."

Micah's tongue stumbled over the words. I took in his hazy eyes and loose jaw. "What did you take?"

"Muscle-relaxy things."

"Relaxy things?"

"Yup. Says so on the box."

Déjà vu hit me. He looked exactly the same as he had that awful day I'd accused him of going on a coke binge. When I'd perfected the art of being a Grade A judgemental arsehole and a terrible friend. *That's not happening again. Ever.*

I helped him sit up and considered our options. Couching it with Netflix was appealing, but if Micah fell asleep again, I didn't want to disturb him to hustle him to bed. Of course I could leave him to sleep in peace, but unless we were sharing a goddamn bed, that wasn't happening. "Can you stand?"

"Huh? Why? Where are we going?"

"My room. We can watch TV and order Chinese."

"You don't like Chinese."

"No, I don't like all that steamed green crap you order. I like fried chicken balls and sweet and sour sauce."

"That's not Chinese food. That's gunk they feed the English."

"What's your point?"

"Can't remember."

I stood and brought Micah upright with me. He seemed surprised by the turn of events but didn't protest as we moved slowly to my bedroom. His legs—plural—weren't working. I half carried him to my bed and eased him down. "Wow. Those meds did a number on you."

Micah evaded my gaze. "I think I took too many."

"You *think*?"

"Yeah. I took three when I shoulda took two. And I forgot to buy more Nurofen, so I figured I needed a bit more."

"You could've asked me to get some painkillers for you. In fact, you could've just asked me where I keep them in the flat."

"You have some?"

"Yes, Micah. It's a pretty common household item."

Though I guessed it had been a long time since Micah had last lived in a regular household. Swanky bachelor pads, flashy cars, and more money than sense didn't seem to come with much self-care and normality.

I left him and fetched a sensible dose of ibuprofen from the kitchen cupboard. When I got back, he was in my bed, stretched out on his side, a pillow tucked under his head like he was a permanent fixture. My heart flipped. We'd had so many conversations about why being together was a bad idea, but none about where we were going as we seemed to be doing it anyway. What if he woke up one day and went back to his own room? Shut the door in my face and stayed there? Micah was by nature unpredictable, unreadable, and thoroughly unreasonable. Was I strong enough to deal if this really did blow up in my face?

Anxiety coursed through me as I realised I had no idea. I loved him so much, and he loved me too, but what if it wasn't enough?

"Sam?"

"Yeah?"

"Stop staring like a weirdo and come keep me warm."

I crossed the room in a heartbeat and slid under the covers. "You're cold?"

"Nah. Just wanted you."

He deposited his head in my lap, his arms loosely around my waist. His eyes drooped shut and I let my hands find their way home to his hair. I wanted more than anything to slide down beside him and doze the night away, but my treacherous imagination wouldn't quit. "Can I ask you something?"

"'Bout what?"

"About your leg. I mean, apart from the other week, has this happened before?"

"Why are you asking me that?"

"Because I want to know if you've been in so much pain you can't walk and I haven't noticed."

Micah sighed. "Why? It's not your job to look after me. Do you know how embarrassing this is?"

"About as embarrassing as that time I came home so drunk I tried to take a piss in the shoe cupboard?"

"Worse. You're cute when you're drunk. I'm a useless heap of shit when I'm like this."

"That's not fair."

"Uh-huh."

"And you didn't answer my question." I rubbed the knots out of his neck. "Though I guess maybe you did with what you didn't say."

"Dude, I'm way too stoned to follow when you say shit like that."

I was talking mostly to myself, but Micah's dazed expression was so comical that a laugh escaped me. It sounded unnatural in the dim quiet of my bedroom, but humour danced in his eyes too, and I knew that, for tonight at least, we'd be okay.

Micah slept through dinner, which was just as well, considering I didn't order the healthy crap he liked and gorged myself on fried dough balls while he rested. I set season five of *Breaking Bad* up on Netflix—I'd promised Micah I'd catch up so we could watch *El Camino* when it came out, but as hooked as I was on Walt and Jesse, it was hard to concentrate on their meth-cooking adventures while Micah was so utterly beautiful beside me.

When I was done eating, I cleared up, filled a plate for him to heat later if he wanted it, and crept back into the bedroom. He was still on his side, head resting on one arm, face buried in my favourite pillow. I reclaimed my space and slid down to his level. His soft hair was forever tempting, but his cheekbones enchanted me. I'd always loved his eyes, but with them hidden by sleep, I wasn't distracted by how troubled they were. I was free to stroke my thumb over his cheek without worry, trail my fingers down his neck, and ghost my palm along his torso.

I was mesmerised. I didn't notice his eyes had slid open until I'd been fixated on his warm skin for a good ten minutes. *Whoops*. I let my hands drop. "Sorry."

"Nah. Don't you dare." Micah grabbed my wrists. "Don't stop. Please don't stop."

I wasn't about to argue.

Micah rolled onto his back, and I resumed my journey across his chest and down to his ripped abs. He so often claimed he was out of shape, but if this was what he looked like after a rough year, there was no way I'd have been able to handle him before.

Not that the state of his abs had much to do with how obsessed I was with him. Micah was ridiculously gorgeous, but it wasn't his fine bones and smooth skin that had captivated me since we'd met. It was his subtle kindness, gentle manner, and sardonic sense of humour. I laughed when he laughed, even when he was taking the piss out of me, and I smiled when he smiled because it was like the sun on a winter morning.

As poetic as all that was, though, I couldn't deny that the waistband of his sweatpants called to me. With his gaze tracking my every move, I fished the jar of coconut oil I used for, er, stuff, out of the bedside table. I straddled him, careful to keep my weight off his legs, and eased his sweats down.

He was already hard, and my blood heated at the sight of him. It seemed like a lifetime had been and gone since the very first time I'd had him so ready and willing for me to touch him like this, and he hadn't let me since. He'd been too obsessed with sucking my dick, and I'd lacked the willpower to protest.

I smoothed the silky oil over my hands. Micah licked his lips, a smirk forming, but it evaporated with his low groan as I closed slick fingers around his cock. He tipped his head back and a full-body shiver shuddered through him.

"*Fuck.*"

"Yeah? You like that?"

"Yeah."

I worked him slowly, torturing myself as much as him, teasing gravelly moans from him, revelling in the spasms that jerked his muscles. Sweat beaded his skin, and a flush crept over his chest. Every part of him moved with my hands, and watching him come undone was the hottest thing I'd ever seen.

He came hard, arching his back from the bed, hands curled in fists around the sheets. "Oh god, oh god."

Sticky warmth coated my hands, but I kept jerking him until he wrenched himself free and yanked me up the bed. "Come in my mouth."

I was powerless to refuse. I pushed my cock between his lips and slid down his throat, my every nerve on fire. I'd never been so turned on in my life, and I'd spent *a lot* of time with my dick in my hand.

Micah's mouth was something else. Hot, tight, and wet, I imagined what it would feel like to fuck him with my cock as slowly as I had with my hands. To slide inside him and make him scream. The mere thought of it was my undoing, too much and yet nowhere near enough. Pleasure sluiced through me, and I came with a strangled yell.

Panting, I climbed off him and collapsed in a heap beside him. The TV had turned itself off and we were in darkness.

Micah found my hand and squeezed. "You broke the relaxy things."

15

Micah

"I want to come with you."

Sam pulled his jeans up his legs and retrieved last night's T-shirt from the floor. "To the library? Again?"

"Yes."

"Why?"

Cos I want to be with you every fucking second before you go to work later. "I like the library."

His face split in half with the kind of smile I hadn't seen from him in weeks. "Really?"

"Yeah. It's all quiet and shit. Like a spa without all the slime they smear on you."

"Sounds like you have experience in such things."

I sat up on my elbows, already resenting the loss of him pressed into my side as we'd slept in his bed. Fucking *mourning* it. "Football clubs have links with swanky health clubs. Lots of players own them too, so you end up having to go and pretend you enjoy that shit so they can put your name on their list of patrons to attract idiots who think it matters."

Sam shook his head. "I'll never understand that life."

"Trust me, you don't want to."

"You don't miss the money?"

"Nope. I miss having something to do every day without having to think about it. And I miss being good at something. But I don't give two fucks about anything else."

"You're good at training other people. I see the progress messages your clients post in that WhatsApp group. They pop up on your screen."

"Yeah, so I can read them without having to go in and reply. I'm a shit trainer because I'm too lazy to properly commit."

"Liar."

He disappeared into his bathroom. I wanted to follow him and push him into the shower so we could have dirty, wet sex, but we weren't there yet. And, despite Sam waiting on me hand and foot for the last twenty-four hours, my leg wasn't up to it. A slow walk to the library was about all I could handle, and only because Sam's presence would distract me from my embarrassing shuffle.

I forced myself out of his bed and took a shower in the other bathroom. When I got out, my phone was ringing. Freddie, obviously; no fucker else ever called me. "'Sup?"

"Not much. Just checking in."

"Why? You wanna hit the gym tomorrow? I'm busy today."

"Yeah, about that."

"About what? Me being busy? I know it's a rare thing, but I do have a life, you know."

"I know. I meant about hitting the gym. I'm gonna have to give it a miss for a while."

"You hurt yourself?"

"Nah."

I paused in the action of jamming my toothbrush in my mouth, belatedly picking up on Freddie's tone. It wasn't like him to be so fucking awkward. That vibe was all mine. "What is it then?"

"It's the club, man. They don't like the attention we're getting. Said it's a distraction we don't need right now. They asked me to stay away from you until the end of the season, in public, at least."

Cold water flooded my chest. "They really said that?"

"Yeah. I mean, they were super careful to stress that it wasn't a gay thing, but it was pretty clear I'm gonna spend the rest of the year on the bench if I get papped getting all handsy with you again."

Handsy. He'd put his fucking arm around me because I'd been angsting over someone else. Because he was my friend. But I guess even that was toxic. *I* was toxic to anyone unfortunate enough to get close to me.

There wasn't much else to say. Freddie said his goodbyes and hung up, leaving me to stare at myself in the mirror and imagine I could see my heart thundering in my chest and the betrayal dripping through me. I didn't blame Freddie for complying with his club or even the bosses for asking him to, but I hated that it hurt me so much. Hated myself for letting it.

Sam knocked on the bathroom door. "Did you get lost in there?"

More than you know.

Sam

Micah was in a mood. He was trying to hide it but failing miserably. And I was failing miserably in my attempts to make him feel better, but for once I didn't blame myself. Micah wasn't like everyone else. Simple things didn't cheer him up, and given that we weren't at home so I couldn't ply him with food until he cracked a smile, I was fresh out of ideas.

We sloped into the library. I'd been planning on taking a desk upstairs and working for most of the day, but with Micah to entertain —or not—I ditched that idea and headed straight for the cavernous fiction section.

Micah trailed behind me while I searched the aisle for something to keep him busy. It took a while, but eventually I shoved a copy of *In One Person* at him and pointed at an armchair. "Go sit."

He grunted and did as he was told.

Rolling my eyes, I left him to it and found a quiet corner on the next floor to practise my essay questions.

The distance between us was deliberate. I was finding it harder and harder to be away from him for any prolonged period of time, but I had exams coming up . . . exams I'd ballsed-up once already. I couldn't afford an entire morning of Micah distraction.

I lost myself in *Frankenstein*, a novel that bored and enthralled me in equal measure. Time slipped away. My stomach growled. I checked my phone: 13:00. *Shit*. I'd left Micah downstairs for three hours.

Cursing, I packed my books and pens away and dashed for the lift. It didn't come. *Fuck it.* I ran to the stairs and jogged down them at breakneck speed. The armchair where I'd left Micah was by the window, behind the true crime section. I half expected to find it empty, a cold cushion where he'd once been, but as I stumbled round the corner, he was still there, legit engrossed in his book.

My herd-of-elephants approach gave my presence away. He glanced up and a ghost of a smile danced on his lips. For a long moment, he simply stared at me while I *gazed* at him.

Then he lifted his arm and gestured for me to sit beside him.

I didn't need asking twice. I dropped my bag and inserted myself into the small space left on the snuggle chair. It was a perfect fit. Micah let his arm fall around my shoulders. I leaned into him and swallowed a ridiculously contented sigh.

In an effort to contain myself, I peeked at his book. "John Irving cracked you, then?"

"A bit. I keep thinking it's boring without you, then another hour goes by and I haven't looked up."

"The magic of a good book."

"Either that or I've got a thing for cross-dressing."

"That right?"

Micah hummed. "Maybe. Whatever. You got me. I like the book."

Victory started a rave in my belly. I'd been waiting for this day since we'd met, or rather, since I'd first realised he was craving a healthy way to detach from reality. My mind immediately jumped to what I could get him to read next.

He tapped my temple. "Stop it."

"Stop what?"

"Driving at a hundred miles an hour. Just enjoy being right for once."

"For once?"

"Yeah. You were wrong about my capacity for words about twenty times."

"Fifteen, actually."

"Whatevs."

Micah went back to his book, and it was the most enchanting thing to watch. I cuddled against him, absorbing his warmth, and enjoyed the most perfect moment we'd ever shared.

Micah

Sam made everything better. One day he'd learn he didn't have to try so hard. That his company was enough. That *he* was enough. And I liked the book, though I still knew jack about wrestling, which would disappoint Freddie if he ever spoke to me again.

The thought stoked the black fire smouldering in my belly. To calm it, I shifted my gaze to Sam. He was leaning against me, eyes closed. If I hadn't known better, I'd have assumed him asleep.

But I did know better. Sam slept like a dead man, smooth-faced and serene. Not with the myriad of thoughts creasing his forehead or the wild animal that was apparently trapped in his stomach.

I nudged him. "Hungry?"

"Huh?" He opened his eyes. "How did you know?"

"Psychic."

"If only."

"What does that mean?"

"That if you could read my mind, you'd have known an hour ago that I'm craving a bowl of pasta from Rosa's."

"I don't need to read your mind to know that. You bring it home twice a week."

"You want to go home?"

It wasn't remotely close to what I wanted. I was as hungry as him, and for once, grabbing takeout and returning to the same four walls, even with him, held little appeal. "I don't want to go home." I reluctantly disentangled myself from him and stood. "I want lunch. Let's go."

I held out my hand. He took it as if I'd grown mutant paws, but I ignored his surprise. I didn't need reminding that we rarely went anywhere together, let alone out for lunch, and the closest we'd come was when I'd brought Freddie into the Fox and Sam had waited on us.

Freddie.

I sighed and tugged Sam's hand. "Come on."

We walked to the all-day Italian bistro that was halfway back to the flat. It was busy with wanker bankers, but we found a table by the kitchen, which suited me just fine. I had no desire to sit near some handjob with an iPad and a bad suit.

Sam passed me a menu and sniggered. "You have such a mean mug."

I couldn't deny it. "People annoy me."

"No, they don't. Your reactions to them annoy *you*."

"That makes no sense."

"Does to me."

"Huh. Maybe it's you that's annoying."

"If you say so."

I didn't. Sam had never annoyed me in his life. It was always, *always* me that irritated—

Fuck.

I threw him a scowl and took the menu. "Stop talking."

He shrugged and dove into his menu for no reason whatsoever as we both knew he'd have the *penne al salmone* like he always did, while I picked my way through the list, trying everything twice.

Oh, the fucking irony.

Still haunted by my encounter with his mum's deep-fat fryer, I chose the broccoli fettuccini with garlic and chilli. My soul cried out for garlic bread and carbonara, but I hadn't hit the gym in days, and sluggish carb comas depressed me.

Depressed me more.

Whatever.

We ordered the food and sat close together, heads bowed as we leaned in like we did at home. Sam smiled. "This is nice. Feels almost normal."

"Normal?"

"Yeah. Like other people. Not that I don't love holing up at home with you."

"Would you go out more if you didn't have me to look after?"

"I don't look after you." Guilt flashed in his gaze. "I've been a proper stroppy fucker for weeks."

I snorted. "One, you sound so fucking Yorkshire right now I can't even. Two, just being there is looking after me. I thought I'd spend the rest of my life alone when I left my club. It was like I'd forgotten how to make friends . . . if I'd ever really known."

"Freddie's your friend. I'm a dick to him because, well, he *is* a bit of a dick, but I know he's a good bloke, really."

"There's more to life than Freddie, or, at least, there should be."

Sam's eyes narrowed a touch. "What does that mean?"

"Nothing."

"Sure about that? Cos you've got your murder face on."

I made an effort to soften my habitual frown.

Clearly unconvinced, Sam rolled his eyes. "Whatever. You don't have to tell me."

"There isn't anything to tell."

Thankfully, our food arrived before Sam could call bullshit, and he was instantly and adorably distracted.

I loved watching him eat almost as much as I was discovering I liked watching him sleep. Life fell away from him, and he was happy. It was a world away from the frantic elation I could bring him with my mouth on his dick, but the contentment in my heart was the same.

And so was the heat in my veins. Yeah, cos I was that kind of perv —watching him eat made me horny.

I shifted in my seat and sought cover in my lunch. The bustle of the bistro agitated me enough to dull my appetite, but I forced the whole plate down. I wasn't gonna fuck this quasi-date up by being a claustrophobic freak.

When we were done—which was approximately three minutes later—he sat back in his seat and eyed the door. "Have you had enough yet?"

"To eat?"

"No, of being out and about. We can go home if you want."

"Unless it's to get naked, I'm good."

Sam's eyebrows twitched. "Uh, that's okay with me, but maybe we should walk the pasta off first, if you're up to it?"

I was up for anything that led to tumbling him to the nearest bed, but my leg was still being an arsehole. I considered our options and our location. "We could get the Tube to Regent's Park? My mum used to take me there when I was little."

"You haven't been since?"

"Not for fun."

"Work?"

"Charity five-a-side," I clarified. "The gym wants me to host boot camps there in the summer too, but I'm ignoring that and hoping it goes away."

Amusement warmed Sam's face again. "That shouldn't be funny, but I get the feeling you'd have been dead against that even before."

"Yeah, and it doesn't make much sense, given that my job was to exercise in public, but there you go. My therapist says I'm a walking contradiction." Meera's face popped into my brain. It had been a while since I'd seen her, and I'd cancelled my last session when my leg had flared up. Maybe later I'd finally get round to rescheduling, but with Sam at my side, it didn't feel that important.

I dropped cash on the table and held out my hand. "Let's walk."

16

Sam

A week of good times and somehow I was still waiting for the sky to fall down. Every morning I woke up with Micah in my bed, ate breakfast with him before we went our separate ways for the day, and met up again at night for snacks and . . . other stuff, and all the while I couldn't shake the sensation that we were existing in some kind of idealistic limbo.

It was as if Micah had forgotten the rest of the world existed. He still went to the gym and did his thing, but other than that, I had his undivided attention. He even started coming to the pub on weekdays and sitting in the corner with his book and ditching his diet Coke for half pints of the ale I'd introduced him to up north. Combined with his designer sports gear, the old-man drink was cute as hell, but the whole situation was . . . strange.

"Are you two seeing each other now?"

I broke my stare with the back of Micah's head as he headed out for the night, and found myself pinned by Céleste. "Of course. We live together. I see him every day."

"So do I now. What's up with that?"

I ignored her and ducked into the storeroom.

She followed me. "Something's happened between you, hasn't it?"

"Nope."

"Liar. Look at you. You're practically glowing."

"Am not. I'm my usual sardonic and cynical self, thank you very much."

"You're neither of those things, especially when it comes to that hunky football player out there."

"Ex-football player."

"Semantics." Céleste stepped closer to me, getting up in my personal space and waving a gelled fingernail in my general direction. "Did you sleep with him?"

"What? No!" At least, not in any sense that didn't involve actually sleeping. Micah was still king of the spontaneous blowjob, and I was working hard at perfecting the art of taking him apart with my hands, but he didn't seem in a hurry to move things along, and I wasn't brave enough to push him. I didn't dare, and perhaps that was what bugged me so much. The fear of getting this far and scaring him off. Micah had always had a home in my heart, but in recent weeks, he'd put down roots and laid the foundations of a love I'd never get over if I lost him.

When. If. When. If.

I focussed on Céleste. "I haven't slept with him."

"But you want to?"

"Course I do. How is that news to you?"

"It isn't, but something's changed, and stop denying it or I'll deck you."

Unfortunately for me, I believed her. I moved to the door and checked the bar. It was packed enough to keep the rest of the staff occupied, but not busy enough that anyone would feel the need to come and find us—the perfect balance for a stockroom gossip.

I shut the door and stood with my back against it. "We haven't had sex, but I guess you could say we're dating? Kind of? Is that even a thing these days?"

"There must be an Instagram term for it, but you're too old for that now."

"I'm twenty-five."

"Exactly. You're not a teenager, so it doesn't need a label. How you feel is more important than what you call it."

"You know how I feel about Micah."

Céleste leaned against a beer barrel. "I know you like him. What I don't understand is how that's escalated to him following you around like a lost puppy while you gaze at him across the bar when you've always given me the impression he's not interested in you that way."

"I didn't think he was."

"What changed?"

"Everything. Nothing. I don't know." I shrugged, devoid of the words to explain me and Micah. "I took him to my parents' place after Valentine's Day for a break. Stuff happened while we were there, and he told me he loved me a few weeks ago."

"He loves you? As in loves you as a friend or wants-to-bang-your-brains-out loves you?"

"The second one, I think."

"You think?"

"Yes. Jesus. Stop questioning everything I say. That part's simple: he loves me, and I love him. It's the rest of it that's complicated."

Céleste's gaze burned with more questions, but she gestured for me to keep talking.

I took a deep breath. "I just don't think he's ready for what comes after the fooling around and wild declarations. He's been through so much, I don't think he trusts himself to love me or believes in himself enough to even try."

"How can that be true if he's already told you he loves you?"

"Because I'm paraphrasing all the shit he comes out with when he's having a bad day."

"And how often is that?"

"Recently? Not so much. At the start, it was all the time, but in the last week or so, things have been pretty perfect."

"The glow." Céleste nodded sagely. "I knew it. You're happy, aren't you?"

Was I? With the disquiet buzzing in my gut, I couldn't be sure, but god, I wanted to be. "I'm trying," I said. "It's just . . . I don't know. I guess I'm scared. I spent so long accepting he'd never want me the way I've always wanted him, maybe I'm having a hard time believing any of this is real. That it's too good to be true."

"Well, I think you're being a whiny drama queen and totally disrespecting Micah by being so down on something that he clearly wants as much as you do."

And there it was: the reason Céleste and I were friends. She had no time for introspective bullshit, and I knew I was about to get a brutal dose of her sharp tongue. "Go on." I closed my eyes. "Do your worst."

"You're taking his insecurities and using them to cover your own."

"Wow."

"It's true. You might be right about everything you've said about Micah, but have you ever considered that it all applies to you too?"

"I haven't been through what Micah has. I have no good reason to be insecure and crippled with self-doubt."

"So?" Céleste barked out loud enough to be heard in the next borough. "Who does? There isn't an entry test for crappy self-esteem. Like, you don't have to pass the personal tragedy exam."

Oh my days, she was really going there. "I don't have self-esteem issues."

"No? Then why don't *you* believe in yourself enough to accept that Micah loves you? Sounds to me like you're vibing off each other's negativity, and if he's as traumatised by what's gone before as you say he is, maybe *you're* the one who needs to fix it. I—"

The stockroom door opened, shoving me forwards. Andy, our much ignored and maligned boss, stuck his head in. "What on earth are you two doing in here? We're getting slammed."

Céleste moved seamlessly to a crate of tonic water. "We were on our way. Sam was digging out the Pepsi syrup before you pushed him over."

Andy knew better than to argue. Céleste had torn him to shreds too many times to count. He ducked back to the bar, leaving me to load up with soda syrups we probably didn't need, and got back to work.

It was another three hours before I left. I'd barely had a moment to consider the bollocking Céleste had given me, and the walk home didn't gift me anymore headspace. But perhaps it was just as well. Overthinking had always been my downfall, anticipating problems that didn't come, catastrophes that never happened.

I let myself into the flat. Micah was in the hallway wearing nothing but sweats and a smirk. I dropped my coat on the floor and beckoned him forwards.

He hesitated only a moment before he lunged at me, and as my back hit the door, I had to consider the possibility that perhaps Céleste had been right.

Maybe that sky fall wasn't going to happen after all.

Micah

I pushed Sam against the front door, eager to kiss away the deep lines of thought he'd brought home. I was tired of being the reason his lovely face creased up. The only grimace I wanted to see from him was when I slid my cock inside him—

Whoa. I fought the image that flashed into my mind. Fucking Sam was the motherload. We weren't there yet . . . were we?

Logic told me no way in hell. That every vow I'd made to myself in the last year—the sensible ones about not thinking with my dick—still held firm, but with Sam squirming in my arms, fighting to strip his clothes and mine, my body said something else.

I want him.

I dragged him off the door and pushed him towards his bedroom. He stumbled, and the animal in me fucking loved it, despite *hating* the fact that I had to limp after him. In my head, I pounced on him, lifted him clean from the floor, and legit threw him down, but the reality was he scooted naked onto the bed while I struggled for enough balance to get my clothes off.

He didn't seem to notice. His gaze was fixed on my dick.

I licked my lips. "See something you like?"

"Yeah."

One loaded syllable was all it took for my pulse to jump through the roof. Heat rushed me, and I manoeuvred myself onto the bed, balancing on my good knee. I brought my cock to Sam's mouth and tapped his lips with the already sticky head. "Open up."

His eyes widened, and I knew why. We'd fooled around loads over the last however long it had been, but not like this. I'd never towered over him, dick in hand, and demanded anything. Demanded *everything*. But I was done playing around. Frightening energy pulsed in my veins, and my hands itched to take his head and jam his mouth down on my cock.

But there was nothing scary about being with Sam. And he didn't need my help to swallow my dick.

He opened up and took me down. I thought I was ready for the sensation of his tongue sliding along my length—I'd been thinking about it all damn day—but I was sorely mistaken. Pleasure shot through me, and I wavered on my one good knee.

I grabbed the headboard for balance. Nails scraped soft pine, and an inhuman groan escaped me. "Fuck. Yeah, like that, like that."

Sam didn't need my instruction any more than he did physical guidance. He went to town on me, deep throating me like a champ. For long minutes, I thought I could take it, then he moaned around me and madness took over.

My leg gave way. I crumpled to one side, bringing Sam with me, clutching his hair like a drowning man. He rose up on his arms and I rolled onto my back, thrusting into his mouth. Release came at me from every corner, but I fought it. Sam had me so fucking hot for him I'd be hard again in ten seconds flat, but I wasn't ready for this to be over. I wanted the first and only time I came tonight to be something different.

Something we'd never done before.

I wanted to fuck him.

I wanted to own him and turn him inside out.

I wanted him to gaze at me the way I was gazing at him right now. To be so full of fucking wonder and desire he couldn't think straight.

Cos I couldn't think straight. Thoughts and wants crashed through my consciousness so fast I couldn't keep up. My brain spun like an out-of-control carousel. I pictured him on his knees, on his back, on his side with me driving into him. I pictured myself fucking him like I had every other bloke who'd crossed my path, and my mind fractured. Splintered, pieces of my soul scattering on the floor. *No, no, no.* I didn't want Sam splayed out for me like a piece of meat while I closed my eyes and wished I was someone else. His gaze was everything, his kiss, his touch. I couldn't fuck him without giving him my whole self, and I didn't know how to do that.

Panic eclipsed the pleasure coursing through my every nerve. I let go of Sam and sucked in a harsh breath that scraped the insides of my lungs. I was flat on my back, but my brain felt sideways, and Sam's room, once comfortably small, closed in on me. Even the ceiling seemed lower.

Attuned as always, Sam pulled back and crawled up the bed. His hands were warm and damp on my face, his gaze searching. Anxious. And so penetrating I couldn't hold it.

I rolled away from him, half falling off the bed. Pain reverberated up my leg, and I welcomed it, losing myself to a time when pain had been my only anchor to the world. When I craved it and needed it to survive. *Damnit.* I'd been through so much therapy, I knew the black thoughts were fleeting. That I'd blink and they'd be gone, but fuck if they didn't scare the shit out of me.

And I still couldn't balance. I jammed my feet into Sam's carpet, fighting for purchase, but none came. The floor tilted up to meet me, and I crashed to my long-suffering knees.

"Jesus!" Sam leapt from the bed and landed like a cat beside me. "What's the matter?"

I barely heard him over the buzzing in my brain. I shook my head to clear it, but it made it worse. Made it louder. Sharper. I couldn't cope.

Groaning, I buried my face in my arms.

Sam swore again and wrestled with me, peeling my arms away. "Hey. Come on. It's okay. What happened? Did something spook you?"

Did it? As Sam pulled me into a bear-like embrace, I suddenly had no idea. My crowded brain emptied itself like a sinkhole had formed at the bottom, and I had no fucking idea what I was doing on his bedroom floor, naked and trembling in his arms. "I—"

Nope. Nothing.

Sam sat down and held me impossibly closer. I hid my face in his chest and breathed him in, desperate for his familiar scent to overwhelm the lingering terror in my gut, all the while searching for the trigger. I'd had inexplicable blackouts before, but not for a long time, and never, ever sober.

And never with Sam. He was my fucking sunshine, even when he left his laundry all over the couch instead of folding it and putting it away. When he left dishes in the sink for days and wet towels on the bathroom floor. *It's not him, it's me.*

Of course it was. It was always me.

I clung to him, breathing deep while he combed his fingers through my hair. I braced myself for more questions, but none came. Perhaps he'd given up on understanding me, or maybe he knew he didn't have to. That whatever weirdness I threw at him, I *loved* him.

The disquiet faded. *I love him, I love him, I love him.* Words were beyond me, but I pressed my face into his chest and prayed he heard me.

One hand still tangled in my hair, Sam reached over me and flicked his Bluetooth speaker on. Some indie band I couldn't place filtered out, all emo lyrics and soft guitars. The melodies were gentle, pretty, almost. But the bass and drums were dark enough to be sexy as hell. Just like him.

I belatedly remembered that he was naked too. And realised that he'd somehow shifted us along the carpet so he was leaning against the bed, me a heap of limbs and emotion in his lap. I gazed up at him and trailed my hand over his cock. It sprung to life against my fingers and he sucked in a breath.

"You don't have to do that."

"I want to."

"Yeah, well, I want to do things to you too, but not if it upsets you."

"You don't upset me. I upset myself."

"Why?"

"I don't know. Sometimes I do, but not this time."

Sam nodded slowly. "Do you trust me?"

"Course I do."

"Sure about that?"

"Yes."

"Would you get on your knees for me?"

"Not on the floor. On the bed, maybe?"

"Do it."

His soft command went straight to my dick. I hauled myself off the floor and scrambled onto the bed. Sam followed and positioned me how he wanted me—on my knees, chest supported by a pillow that smelt of him. Of us, actually, as we rarely slept on the same side of the bed two nights in a row. He widened my legs, somehow knowing the exact position that was easiest on my damaged leg.

I felt no fear as he moved behind me, only the prickly heat of anticipation. *Does he want to fuck me?* I'd only bottomed once, years ago when a coke-fuelled hook-up had got out of hand. I'd been too off my nut to realise the dude had—unintentionally—hurt me, and pre-season training had started the day after.

I shivered.

Fun times.

Sam rubbed my back. He didn't say anything, but he didn't have to. I wasn't bent up like this for talking, but I knew him well enough to know he wouldn't try and cram his dick inside me without a conversation, and—

"Holy *shit!*"

Sam swept his tongue over me, gently at first, but then with more purpose when I didn't object.

As if I could. Fucking hell, it was incredible. Teasing strokes interspersed with probing licks stole my power of speech. Stole everything except the ability to simultaneously shiver, dribble, and moan.

The pleasure was insane. Not enough to make me come, but just enough to remind me that I'd fall off the edge of the world when I did.

I arched my back, desperate for friction. "Fuck, fuck, fuck."

"Yeah? You like that?"

I mourned the sudden loss of his mouth on me. "Don't stop. Please. Don't ever stop."

He took pity on me and resumed his slow torture, and I went back to falling apart in the sweetest way. Minutes went by, maybe even hours, I had no clue. All I knew was that I'd combust if we carried on like this, and I didn't fucking care. *I wanna burn for him.* Fire crept through me, singeing every negative thought in its path, a temporary cure for a permanent problem. In the back of my mind, I knew the moment he stopped, I'd be right back where I'd started, but for every second he had his tongue in me, I was a better man. A happy man. A man who could only sob with pleasure as the love of my life took me apart.

Sam reached around me and took my cock in his hand. A featherlight squeeze was all it took. With his tongue still sweeping into me and his fingers around my dick, I was so undone. I convulsed, let out a strangled yell, and came like a fucking freight train.

More sounds fell from my lips as I made a mess of his bed, but I didn't care about that either. I toppled forwards into the pillow, half laughing, half who the fuck knew what. Sam caught me before I faceplanted and turned me around. His eyes seemed to flicker as he stared at me. "All right? You're okay?"

I offered him a dazed smile and shrugged. Because I was okay.

For now.

17

Sam

Life was weird. One minute I was angsting over, well, everything. The next I was being swept off my feet by Micah at any given opportunity. Sometimes literally—he'd developed a thing for swinging me around the kitchen—other times, it was more subtle.

Like the day he finished his book and bounced into my bathroom to tell me all about it. "I wanna be in my sixties and not give a fuck."

"Give a fuck about what?"

"Anything."

I poked my head around the shower curtain. "You'll have to be more specific. I never actually got through that book. I was spoiled by *The Hotel New Hampshire*."

Micah shot me a blank look.

"One of his other books."

"Oh," he said. "Well I liked this one. It was weird as fuck, and I was kinda rooting for Billy to hook up with a bloke, but I liked that he didn't too. Does that make sense?"

"That you appreciated the fact that a queer character wasn't shoehorned into every possible facet of their sexuality? Yes, it makes sense. You'd still be bi if you'd only been with women, right?"

"Yeah. I definitely like it all."

I tried to contain my smirk. There was something truly fucking erotic about knowing that Micah saw the possibility of attraction in everyone, even if the mere thought of him with someone else made me want to bleach my brain. *Needy?*

Totally.

"Uh, Sam?"

"Hmm?" I blinked to find Micah closer than he'd been before, hovering by the bathtub, frowning. "What? What is it?"

"Can I get in the shower with you?"

"Of course." I stepped back to make room. "You don't have to ask."

Micah stripped his clothes and climbed into the shower. The en suite to my room was the most modern room in the flat, complete with a raindrop shower head that was wide enough to keep us both wet and warm. Micah backed me against the tiles and wrapped his arms around me. Jitters danced under his smooth skin, but his stance was relaxed, and with his face buried in my neck, I couldn't gauge his breathing under the hot spray. Was he agitated? Or just horny? Over the last week, I'd struggled to tell the difference. Subtle shifts in Micah's personality had thrown me for a loop. No longer on the sullen side of quiet, he was louder, chattier, and come the evening . . . drinking. Not a lot, but it was so brand new to me I didn't know what to make of it.

Maybe he's just happy.

If only. But, alas, nothing about Micah was ever that simple. When his mood was up, I loved hearing him laugh as though the world wasn't pressing down on him. When he was like this, he scared me. His moods were giving me whiplash. I couldn't imagine how it felt for him—to be so carefree one moment and riddled with anxiety the next. It was as if the lid to his emotions had been lifted and they were all escaping at once, and the worst thing about it was he seemed to have no idea.

I held him until the water ran cold. Then he blinked a slow smile at me, climbed out of the shower, and wandered off. I caught up with him a few minutes later. He was on the couch, dressed, hair still dripping, towel in an uncharacteristic heap on the floor. I made tea and dumped it on the coffee table before flopping down beside him. "What are you doing today?"

"Hmm?" Micah glanced up from flipping cutely through his book. "Oh, I dunno. What time is it?"

"Nine. Do you have clients? I thought you'd be gone when I woke up."

"I rescheduled my morning."

"Why?"

He shrugged. "I wanted to finish my book."

How could he be so endearing and mystifying at the same time? The Micah I knew was so committed to his clients he dragged himself to the gym when he had the flu. Sat up till late writing training plans and researching rheumatoid arthritis so he could best serve his favourite elderly clients. He didn't blow them off for a book that still had a week on its lending term.

I sipped tea and tried not to let my imagination run away with me. Making assumptions about Micah had lit a fire beneath us before, and not the good kind. I tried to focus on what hadn't changed, namely how sinfully beautiful he was—his dark hair and liquid eyes, his gorgeous skin and strong body.

More than that, his innocent smile when he caught me looking at him.

"What?"

My turn to shrug. "Nothing. Just eyeing you up."

"You're stocktaking at ten."

"So?"

"So you don't have time for whatever you're thinking about."

"I wasn't thinking about anything in particular, only you." It was true, but he was also right about the time. Stock checks at the pub happened every week, but every couple of months, we got roped in for a deep count, and this round, I'd caught the short straw: a double shift scheduled immediately after. I'd be at work for approximately fifteen hours, and even if Micah fucked me six ways from Sunday before I left, I'd never be in the mood for that nonsense.

With a reluctant sigh, I hauled myself from the couch and sloped off to get dressed. For a moment, I thought I heard Micah follow me, but when I got to my bedroom, I was alone.

I threw clothes on—jeans and the only T-shirt I was prepared to spend a whole day in at work and risk being ruined. Placebo hadn't been my bag since 2010 when I'd been a thrilling combination of hormones, rainbows, and angst.

Whistling, I searched my bedroom floor for socks clean enough to pass. Like magic, Micah appeared in the doorway with a balled-up pair. He tossed them to me, looking guilty. I frowned. "What's the matter?"

"That's your only clean pair. I forgot to do the washing."

"It's not your job to wash my clothes, babe."

He flushed like he always had when I used that particular term of endearment, even before we'd started fooling around. It didn't seem to matter that I used it for the handful of people I actually liked and not just for him. "Yeah, but still. You *always* forget, and I don't want you to have no clean socks."

"I have clean socks. You just gave them to me. Feel free to crawl around my bedroom floor and find all my dirty ones, though."

Micah stepped into the room.

I blocked him. "Don't you dare. I was joking."

"How am I going to wash them if you won't let me have them?"

"The same way you always do, by digging them out of the couch."

He rolled his eyes and ambled away. The exchange had been so familiar I could've written our words down before we'd said them. And yet somehow, I still felt like I'd had a conversation with a stranger. Had our physical relationship really altered our friendship that much? Or was I being an angst queen again when all Micah wanted to do was get back to normal?

With blowjobs, obviously.

And declarations of love.

And sleeping side by side every night as if we'd done it a thousand times.

I considered what my life would be like if Micah really did wake up one day and want things to go back to how they'd been before—when we'd been roommates who ate dinner together, talked about the weather, and watched crap films until one of us fell asleep. When we'd hugged goodnight every time I'd been too drunk to resist, and he'd humoured me with the kind of bear hug that kept me up all night. Life had been good then. Easy, maybe. Now, simple things like clean socks gave me a migraine, but there was a Micah shaped imprint in my bed—and my heart—and I'd die before I gave it up.

Micah

Mr Chan was my favourite client. He always showed up on time, trained hard, and spoke only when I asked him to. Sometimes he brought me noodles his wife had made too, glass ribbons with peanuts and chilli. It said a lot of how I felt about Sam that I often saved him half. Those noodles were good.

It was mid-afternoon. I led Mr Chan around the gym, pushing his elderly body to the limit, impressed, as ever that he could still shift fifty kilos on the leg press and smash out supersets of bodyweight pull-ups. He was a fucking unit, and watching him train often hypnotised me to the point where our hour session passed in the blink of an eye.

Not today, though. Today I had ants in my veins and time had slowed to a painful crawl. I clock-watched and drummed my fingers on every available surface—the wall, the mat, the weight rack, even my own head when there was nothing else within reach, the fraught rhythm tapping into my brain until I couldn't keep still.

Mr Chan brought his dumbbells back to the rack and nodded at my fluttering fingers. "Restless? Wife at home waiting?"

And that was the other reason I liked him: he had zero clue who the hell I was and asked me three times a week how my wife was, despite the fact that I'd told him a hundred times that I didn't have one.

I didn't feel like repeating the conversation today. I cut my losses and nodded. "Yup. Hot date."

As if. I'd never been on a hot date in my life, unless you counted heading home to Sam with a pizza and bad intentions. Or my ill-fated Grindr nights out. My mind took flight to what a hot date with Sam would be like. We'd done the eating out thing—*once*—and the cinema was whack when I could watch movies with him at home, in private. Maybe we could go away, get one of those cabins in the woods, and fuck in front of a cute little fireplace. Did Sam like the great outdoors?

Shamefully, I had no idea. I didn't even know if *I* liked it, as the closest I'd ever got to the wilderness was Watford. Everyone thought that travelling with a top-flight football club was all glamorous and shit, but I'd never travelled for fun. I didn't know how.

Mr Chan's session came to an end. I walked him to the changing rooms and retrieved my phone from my locker. Sam had sent me a literary meme I didn't understand, and I had an email from my old club and a couple of messages from Freddie I deleted without reading. I ignored the email too. I could forgive Freddie toeing the line to keep his game alive, but the rest of them could go fuck themselves.

I opened up a Google search for log cabins in the woods. Then got instantly distracted by log burners and wondering if one day Sam would want to move to a place with a garden, with me, and my heart took off at a hundred miles an hour, finally catching up with the galloping brain I'd woken up with that morning. We already lived together, but I was basically his lodger. What would it be like to choose somewhere new together? What if we left London? Or moved back to his hometown? To Whitby? The place where time had seemed to stop and it had just been me and him?

And his parents and their deep-fat fryer. I could still smell the chips.

More than that, I could still feel the sea spray on my face, taste the salt, and if I closed my eyes, the sensation of Sam's hand tucked in mine warmed me to the bone.

"Micah?"

I blinked. The gym's receptionist was in front of me, a young dude whose name I could never remember, but the sensation of an unfinished conversation still lingered between us. "What?"

"Sorry. I thought you'd fallen asleep. You told me not to let you do that again."

Ah. That was it. When I'd first scored PT space at the gym, I'd been so fucking tired of life, I'd have a kip in the corner of the changing room, slumped against the lockers like a drunk old man, just to escape for a few minutes. After a while, though, I'd figured it wasn't a good look and recruited desk dude to supervise me. Larry? Barry? Fucked if I knew.

I sat up and rubbed my eyes. Had I been asleep? That I didn't know disturbed me, but I wasn't about to admit it to someone I didn't know well enough to remember his name.

It's not his fault you have a brain like a sieve. Ask him.

But I couldn't bring myself to do that either. So I didn't. I plucked the first thing that wandered into my mind instead and blurted it out. "I'm looking for a log cabin."

Dude raised a brow and I finally noticed the name tag pinned to his shirt. Everyone who worked here wore one, even me, which was a blast when someone thought they recognised me and contorted themselves into a triangle trying to read the badge I deliberately pinned upside down.

Whatever. Dude's name was Danny. So much for Barry and Larry. And he was staring at me like someone who'd repeated a question a hundred times and was still waiting for an answer.

Again, the sensation of slowly drowning hit me. My ears buzzed, and the room tilted. At least, I thought it did. Then I blinked and everything was as it should've been.

I focussed on Danny and sifted through my brain for the fragments of conversation I'd clearly missed. *Log cabin. Scotland. Newspapers.*

What?

I gave up and shook my head. "Sorry. Spaced for a minute. What did you say?"

Danny opened his locker and tossed a red top at me. "I said my sister spent her honeymoon at a retreat in Inverness. It's so remote you can't find it online. They only advertise old-school style in the back of the newspapers. I dunno which ones, but you might get lucky with this one."

I caught the paper and turned it over in my hands as Danny left the room. It felt good to be alone again, but at the same time, solitude was terrifying, and I couldn't deal with the conflict raging in my chest. I didn't understand it. I'd felt like this for days, elated one moment—and so fucking in love—only to be so needy and scared the next that it was all I could do not to bolt from the changing room and run all the way down the road to where Sam was working at the pub. Perhaps Meera could've explained it or helped me explain it to myself, but I'd let my appointments lapse, and she was fully booked now until the end of the month.

Idiot. Missing therapy appointments had never panned out well for me in the past. Right now, I didn't have the kind of brain that could handle being left unsupervised so long. *Call her. Tell her you need to see her.*

But the only calls I'd made in the last few weeks had been to Sam.

The image of him and me stretched out naked and fucking in front of an open fire filled my head again. Angst forgotten, I opened the paper. Knife crime and sensationalised celebrity gossip bombarded me like a bad smell. I moved to flick through it to the ad pages at the back, but a headline caught my eye.

"Gay Footballer Finally Goes Public With Roommate Romance!"

Time seemed to stop, along with my perception of reality. For a long moment, I honestly thought it was talking about someone else. Some other poor fuck who'd had his sexuality exploited by the media. Another daft sod who was head over heels in love with his roommate. But no. It was me. For the second time in as many years, my entire life was laid bare for all to see.

And so was Sam's.

18

Sam

Micah burst into the pub, eyes feral, clutching a stack of newspapers. His hoodie was undone and flapping wildly behind him, and his hair was twisted like he'd done everything in his power to yank it out at the roots.

To anyone who hadn't clicked on the link my mum had just sent me, he probably looked like he'd escaped a day-release programme, but I knew exactly what had put that look on his face. I'd just spent ten minutes locked in the stockroom, reading every damning word. Article after article. Hundreds of pictures. Some douchebag pap had been trailing him for months. Trailing *us*. They'd even followed us to Whitby and hung around the pub to catch a snap of me mooning over Micah long before anything had ever happened between us. They were probably still watching us even now.

The door slammed shut behind Micah. He stumbled forwards and crashed into an empty chair. The commotion alerted every soul in a five-mile radius, and Céleste—who'd been with me in the stockroom, obviously—moved fast to intercept him. She caught his arm and towed him away from the main dining area. The alcove was the nearest private place, but it was still way too exposed for my liking.

I caught her eye and pointed to the fire exit. She nodded and disappeared, taking Micah with her while I finished serving the early evening queue.

"He's that gay footballer," my customer supplied helpfully. "I heard he was in the nuthouse. Surprised to see him round here."

Fury built in my chest so fast and sudden I couldn't contain it. I slammed a pint glass down on the bar. "Mind your own fucking business."

I made my escape before I decked someone. Heart thumping, I abandoned the bar and ducked out of the fire exit. Céleste had Micah cornered by the bins. He was pacing like a caged animal, still clutching the newspapers, but at least the high fence protected us from view.

Unless that wanker pap is stalking us from an upstairs window.

Fifteen minutes ago, I'd have laughed at something so ridiculous, but in the cool light of the early evening, anything seemed possible.

Céleste disappeared. I took her place and faced Micah down. "I've seen it. My mum sent me the link."

Micah stopped pacing. "The link to what?"

"The article in *The Sun.* I'm guessing it's in that piece of crap too?" I gestured to the *Daily Mirror* at the top of his pile.

Micah flung the whole lot in my general direction. Pages separated and fluttered messily to the ground. "It's fucking everywhere. That cunt even followed us to the library. Papped us sitting in the chair."

I carried that scene in my dreams, those precious minutes we'd spent leaning against one another, reading, staring, aware of nothing but each other and words on the page. It'd been as close to perfect as I'd ever dared imagine, and I could barely contemplate that it had been stolen from us. I had to see it with my own eyes.

Some of the pages Micah had scattered had landed in a puddle of stale beer leaking from a discarded barrel. I knelt beside it and gathered them up, leafing through them until I found the article. The pictures were grainy and blurred. Nausea rising, I found my phone and pulled up the tabloid's gossip site.

The pictures of us were all over it—having lunch in the bistro, walking in Regent's Park, even holding hands on the train home to Yorkshire. The library pics were further down, perhaps because whoever had taken them had deemed them less interesting than Micah shoving chips in my mouth on Whitby seafront, but they had no idea. Seeing them tossed around the internet was so violating I actually gagged. *Jesus. No wonder he was so poorly after last time.*

I stood to find Micah had moved as far away from me as it was possible for him to be without actually leaving. He'd flattened himself against the fence, jaw set, gaze fixed on the ground. I laid a cautious hand on him.

He flinched.

My heart broke. "Micah. It's okay. It's just some gossip. It'll be tomorrow's chip paper."

"It doesn't work like that."

"Sure it does. There's always new headlines. Okay, it might take more than a couple of days, but they'll get bored."

"They won't. Dom's boyfriend is in the papers all the time. They follow him to work, just like they followed you."

I'd forgotten about that. "Shit."

Micah sighed. "I know, right? I'm so fucking sorry."

"What for?"

"For bringing this bullshit into your life. It's not like I didn't know this would happen, especially after they caught me with Freddie."

"You weren't doing anything with Freddie."

"I wasn't doing anything with you either until they tracked us to your parents' place."

"Uh, they actually papped us on the train. When you were asleep and holding my hand."

Micah closed his eyes. "Come home with me?"

"I can't. I have to work." It was the hardest six words I'd ever uttered, but I needed my job too much to walk out in the middle of a shift. My stockroom meltdowns had me on thin ice as it was. "I'm sorry."

Micah opened his eyes. The haze of anxiety had been there for days, but the burning embers of pure panic seared my soul.

"Micah—"

"Don't." He caught my hands as I reached for him and pushed me away. "I can't handle you being nice about this. It's bullshit."

"It's not your fault."

"Isn't it? If I hadn't blown all my money, I'd never have turned up in your life and wrecked it—"

"*That's* fucking bullshit," I snapped. "Are you seriously saying you'd be better off if you hadn't met me? You realise most of your drama happened before, right?"

Micah's expression collapsed. "Dude, I meant *you'd* be better off."

"Don't fucking 'dude' me." I reached for Micah again, but he turned away before I could comfort him and, despite his dragging leg, slipped through the gate and out onto the street. Given the circumstances, chasing him or shouting him down wasn't an option.

With a heavy sigh, I trudged back inside, leaving the soggy evidence of our entwined lives behind.

Sam

The night wore on and didn't get any better. On my break, I logged into my neglected Twitter account and dropped onto a damp bench with my head in my hands. Me and Micah were trending, in London at least, and there were even more pictures circulating than on the gossip sites. On the plus side, the queer community was raising hell that Micah—that both of us—had been so cruelly exposed, but their righteous anger didn't change much.

I clicked on tweet after tweet of me and Micah together. Some of them appeared so innocuous I was almost amused, but as I looked closer, I realised that every shot told a story, even if we hadn't known it at the time. In one, we'd been caught in the pub's outdoor smoking area. Micah was on his way out, and I was waving goodbye. His smile was electric, and I looked so happy I barely recognised myself.

My heart ached. If I ignored the barbaric violation of our privacy, it was beautiful.

But there had been nothing beautiful about the raw horror in Micah's face when he'd hurled the newspaper at me. Any joy he may have found in how he felt about me—and by default, about himself—had been stolen from him.

Again.

I went back to work, counting the minutes till my shift ended. Andy asked me to stay late and help clean the ale lines. I told him to get fucked, in my head, at least. Out loud, I told a lie about an exam in the morning and left. I ran home, sensing eyes on me as I passed the handful of pubs and bistros that still had customers lingering outside. It was probably all in my head, but my skin crawled nonetheless, and I breathed a sigh of relief when I reached my building.

Inside, I took the stairs two at a time and burst through the front door like a man possessed.

Micah was waiting for me in the hallway. There was no music on, no scent of toasted sandwiches filtering out of the kitchen.

I dropped my bag and coat on the floor, half expecting him to step around me and pick them up like he'd done so many times. But he didn't move. Just stared at me with hollow eyes. "A photographer followed me home," he said flatly. "And they've been camped out across the road ever since. Did they get you?"

"I didn't notice anyone."

"That doesn't mean shit."

His aggression got under my skin. "So, if they did pap me, it's my fault for not paying attention?"

"*No*, it means they'll take advantage of the fact that you're not paying attention and rinse your life until you're as fucking nuts as I am."

"You're not nuts. Don't say things like that."

"Don't fucking tone police me." But the fire had faded from

Micah's voice, and his full bottom lip stuck out like it always did when he was in a bad mood.

I eyed it, wishing I could run my thumb along it. There'd been times when I'd found his sulky expression endearing, funny, even, but I'd left my sense of humour on the proverbial bus. I wanted this to go away. For everything that had hurt him so much to have happened to someone else, and for him to have lived a life that let him brush this off and go back to the bubble that had surrounded the flat, protecting him—and us—from the outside world.

Wishful thinking got me nowhere, though. Micah was still a statue in the hallway, and I was still tired, hungry, and craving his affection.

I toed my shoes off and made a grab for his hand. "Come on. Let's have supper."

He didn't protest as I dragged him into the kitchen, but he stopped short at the stool he usually sat on while I cooked. "Don't. I'll do it."

I shrugged. If he wanted to make me dinner, I wasn't about to stop him. "Lots of mustard."

He even smiled a little. "I know."

Silence fell over us as Micah made sandwiches of slightly stale bread, ham, and the last of the cheese. He dug the extra hot mustard out of the fridge and slathered it on. My mouth watered. Whatever else was going on, no one could take this from us.

He squished them in the sandwich press and toasted them to perfection, two rounds for me, one for him that I already knew he wouldn't eat. Fear flared in my chest. The Micah I knew was guarded by nature, but this was something else. He was shutting down, piece by piece, and there was nothing I could do about it.

I dug into my food, gamely shovelling it in, piling it on top of the despair layered in my gut. Micah stayed quiet, and the bottom of my plate came too soon. I pushed it away. "Look," I said. "Perhaps we just have to accept it's part of our normal now. You said it yourself they're not going to go away, so maybe we can learn to live with it."

Micah's hand slammed down on the counter, making me jump as

much as the plate that skittered across the marble. Rage exploded on his face. He caught the plate and chucked it across the room. It crashed against the doorframe and broke into too many pieces to count. "Don't you understand?" he shouted. "It doesn't matter how many versions of this conversation we have, nothing about this will ever be fucking normal!"

He wheeled away, gone in a flash.

The slam of the front door shattered my heart.

19

Micah

I woke up in a hotel room, buried under the covers of a bed that smelt of other people. The blackout curtains were drawn, shutting the world out, but I was still here, still noisy and broken and heartsick without Sam stretched out beside me. My only consolation was the hotel I'd stumbled into was obscure enough that no one had noticed me checking in. Somehow I'd managed to get past the pap loitering outside the flat.

Time passed in unknown intervals. I slept a lot—so much it scared me. I sunk into the mattress like cat piss on a brand-new couch, and I just . . . didn't care that I couldn't find the energy to move. My leg throbbed—I'd hoofed it for miles before I'd found the hotel—but I welcomed the pain. For however long I lay on that bed, stewing in my own misery, the cramp in my muscles kept me alive.

My phone was somewhere in the bed. It's vibrating and flashing seemed far away, and I didn't care about that either. I missed sessions at work and the last minute cancellation appointment I'd scored with Meera. I forgot to eat and avoided the hotel bathroom with its giant, soul-destroying mirror. I didn't need to see my sallow skin and sunken eyes to know that I was seriously losing my fucking shit.

I'd never felt so unhinged. Even my skull seemed to belong to someone else. It buzzed and zapped, and my fingers tingled with electricity. I lay on my stomach, crushing them with bodyweight, but it was no good. The tingling spread up my arms and into my shoulders and crept up my neck to join the pulsing nightmare in my brain.

New fear seized me. I rolled out of bed. *I have to get out of here.* Gasping, I scrambled for the hotel room door, but my leg gave out, and I hit the floor. For long minutes, I lay there, chest heaving. The room grew dark and then light again, but I couldn't contemplate what it meant. Was I losing whole days to a panic attack on the floor? Or was there something wrong with the lights?

Maybe it was me and my skewed perception of my surroundings. My heart ached for Sam. Voices cried out in my head, screaming his name. I needed him so badly it scared me more than anything, but I couldn't have him. I couldn't be near him while I was like this. On top of everything I'd already put him through, I couldn't let him see me so fucking messed up. *Like he doesn't already know.*

Groaning, I hauled myself to my knees and crawled back onto the bed. Terror still pounded in my chest, cold sweat trickling down the side of my face. *I'm so scared.* Confused too. I hadn't felt this bad in a long time—so sad and overstimulated. The two phenomena warred with each other, fear keeping me awake, while desperate grief kept me prone on the bed. It was the evilest fucking thing.

Go home. Sam will make it better.

But I couldn't. I couldn't move. All I could do was burrow further into the mattress and wish I could sleep forever.

Sam

I had spent many nights staring at my bedroom ceiling and trying to remember what my life had been like before Micah.

I'd never succeeded. When we'd been roommates with unspoken feelings, his quiet presence in my life had been so absolute it had seemed as if he'd always been there. That his soft wit and gentle ways had been my constant companions forever. But reality was a cruel mistress, and his empty bedroom a stick she used to beat me. In the three days since Micah had left, I'd steered clear of it but had somehow felt unable to shut the door. So it stayed open, and his unmade bed taunted me, as if it was a symbol of something I'd yet to decipher, and the longer Micah was gone, the less chance I had of figuring it out.

It didn't make any sense. I mean, on the surface, it did—Micah freaking out because the media had exposed us and removing himself from the situation to spare me the scrutiny. That, I got, but what I didn't understand was why he'd been so volatile and vulnerable leading up to this bullshit. He'd had months and months of therapy to help him deal with the fallout of the last time it had happened. Therapy he attended like church and took super seriously. But if anything, in the weeks before the media clusterfuck, he'd been more out of sorts than ever. Why? Had something happened I didn't know about? Had he stopped going to therapy? Had his medication stopped working?

I sat up in bed and reached for my phone. WhatsApp was already open. Over the past few days, I'd sent Micah many messages. He'd read them all—which reassured me he was alive—but hadn't replied. The last time he'd been online was hours ago, around lunchtime, when I'd sent him a pleading message to talk to me. That we could fix anything if he'd just come home. His silence had hurt more than a red-hot poker to my chest.

You don't understand. You haven't lived his life, and you don't have the mental health issues he does.

True. But I was still human, and him leaving me had broken my heart. Did he really think he could solve this by ducking out on me? That his feelings for me would evaporate the moment we were apart? If it spared him the pain I was in now, I honestly hoped they would. Micah had suffered enough.

I put my phone down and slid out of bed. My bare feet padded on my bedroom carpet until I hit the cool wood of the hallway. I stopped at Micah's bedroom door. His room smelt faintly of him—clean cotton and wood—but the usually tidy space was in disarray, perhaps like his mind. Clothes littered the floor, and there were dirty glasses on the bedside table.

Against my better judgement, I stepped over the threshold to grab them. If he ever came home, he wouldn't like the mess. I took the glasses to the kitchen and returned to make the bed. Clothes found their way to the hamper, and I straightened his chest of drawers, dusting the top and tucking wayward T-shirts back where they came from.

The top drawer was half open. I stood from my crouch to close it, but as I slid it along the runners, I stopped short and opened it again.

Micah's medication was tucked amongst his socks. I remembered him taking it the morning after the first night we'd spent together. How he'd shyly tried to hide it, then changed his mind and met my gaze with a defiance that made my soul bleed.

I couldn't recall seeing him take it since. *What if—*

No. Micah was committed to his recovery. It didn't fit that he'd stop taking his medication any more than he'd dip out on his therapy. *But if he did, these drugs have serious withdrawal symptoms, right?*

I grabbed the packets and laid them out on the top of the chest of drawers. The anti-depressants were a brand name I recognised, but I had no idea what the others were. I couldn't even pronounce the name. But the mystery pills came in a calendar strip, like birth control pills. The last pill had been taken on a Tuesday.

The first night I'd slept in his bed had been a Monday . . . I was sure of it.

There was a football season planner pinned to Micah's bedroom wall. I flicked back to the previous month and found the date. A Monday. Was it possible that he hadn't taken his meds since then?

I didn't want to believe it, but it made sickening sense. His erratic moods and strange behaviour. The emotions he couldn't seem to control—fear, joy, anger. We'd shared some beautiful moments, but I wasn't so blinkered by love that I'd missed the crippling sadness weighing him down. Had he stopped his meds on purpose? Would he do that? I had no idea. In fact, the only thing I was certain of was unless Micah had left the flat with spare pill packets shoved in his pockets, he still wasn't taking them.

Shit.

The dread that had been roiling inside me increased tenfold. Everyone I knew who'd been treated with anti-depressants had been warned not to stop taking them suddenly. That withdrawal syndrome was brutal and dangerous. I typed the name of the other drug into Google. It was a mood stabiliser used to treat severe depression, acute mania, and bipolar disorder. Withdrawal side effects included agitation, restlessness, poor sleep and appetite, and an abrupt return of the symptoms it had been prescribed to treat.

My heart sank. Micah had always kept his official diagnosis close to his chest, and I'd never pushed him, even after we'd grown close enough to share a bed every night, but I couldn't deny that I recognised the symptoms on the screen. I'd seen them. Felt them. And the idea of him out there in the city, dealing with them all alone, scared me to hell.

You don't know that he's alone.

But I did. Freddie was Micah's only real friend, and he was away, playing European football in Germany. I'd seen it on the big screen in the pub.

With shaky fingers, I swiped out of the internet search and called Micah. I got his voicemail, but I hung up without leaving a message and called again, and again, and again, until the line finally crackled to life.

"Micah?"

Rustling and then a heavy sigh. "What?"

Relief flooded me. It wasn't exactly a welcome hello, but after days and days of silence, it was progress. "I'm glad you picked up. Are you okay?"

"Yeah."

"Sure about that? You've been gone a while."

"Sorry."

"Don't be sorry. I just need to know you're safe, Micah. I've been worried about you."

"I'm safe."

Are you sure? Where are you? Have you eaten? But instinct told me to tread softly, so I swallowed the barrage of questions down. "Listen," I said. "I've been wondering about what had got you so restless, even before the paparazzi sold those pictures of us. Do you think it's possible you haven't been taking your medication properly? That you've missed a few doses?"

"What?"

"Your medication," I repeated. "I was in your room putting clothes away, and I found the boxes. It doesn't look like you've touched them for a while."

More rustling, a thud, and then a silence that stretched so long I thought my heart would break my ribs. "Micah? Are you there?"

"I'm here. Fuck—" He coughed like an old man. Drew a sharp, pained breath. Then a gravelly, tortured groan shattered the heavy air between us. "The fuck are you even talking about?"

"Your medication. The anti-depressants and the other pills. I think you forgot to take them."

Silence. Another groan. And then, "I need to sleep."

He hung up.

I stared at the phone in disbelief and called him straight back, but he didn't answer. On my third try, he switched his phone off.

Frustration coursed through me, along with an abrupt certainty that I was right about the pills. Perhaps he'd done it on purpose, but it didn't matter anymore. He'd said he was safe. My heart wanted to believe him, but how could I when his medication was still untouched in his drawer and he was who-the-hell-knew where? *What do I do? Call the police? Freddie? His old club?* I'd never felt so helpless in my life.

My phone rang. I jumped. *Micah*. But when I looked at the screen, it wasn't him. And I answered the phone with a heavy sigh. "Ma, this isn't a good time."

There was rustling at my mum's end, and then her voice, high pitched and scared. "Sam? Can you hear me, son? I need you to come home."

20

Micah

The idea of sleeping forever was cute but farfetched. Too soon, awareness returned to me with a sharp kick in the nuts. I couldn't say how long I'd hibernated under a duvet that smelt of other people, but it was light outside when I forced myself to face the air-conditioned chill of the room.

My brain vibrated. Or maybe it was my phone again. I picked it up and squinted at the screen, but it was blank. Dead battery? Or maybe I'd turned it off. I couldn't remember. Sam's call had turned my head upside down. So many thoughts. I couldn't catch them all.

I slid off the bed and limped to the bathroom. The mirror taunted me. I stepped up to it and caught sight of myself for the first time in days. *Jesus.* My face was a mask of pallid skin and shadowed eyes. Stubble darkened my jaw, but not the sexy kind. It looked like a battered Brillo pad.

Scratch that. *I* looked like a battered Brillo pad.

I leant against the counter and forced myself to retrace however long it had been since I'd last touched base with reality. Sam's call played on repeat. *Medication, medication, medication.* I pictured the white boxes in my top drawer and tried to remember the last time I'd opened them up and popped the pills that plugged the hole in my sanity. The leak in my head caused by years of suppressing who I really was. Meera said I wouldn't need them forever, but maybe she was wrong. Maybe they were the only thing standing between where I was now and where I'd been when I'd first realised Sam loved me back.

Fuck. Sam. I missed him so much. I couldn't think about him for too long. But his phone call haunted me. It didn't matter which way I looked at it, I couldn't remember taking those damn-fucking pills. And I certainly hadn't taken them since I'd made the impulsive decision to run out on him and spend money I needed for the rest of my life on a dank hotel room.

The meds were supposed to stop me making stupid decisions. They were supposed to stop me overreacting to my moods and give me the stability I needed to recover from the crisis that had brought me face to face with an oncoming train. But they couldn't work if I didn't take them, and the harder I thought about it, the more certain I became that I hadn't. My morning routine had gone to shit since I'd started sleeping with Sam. I'd been too distracted by the magic of being so close to him. I didn't regret a moment we'd spent together, but fuck, fuck, *fuck,* I'd messed up.

I backed away from the counter and retreated from the bathroom. My own idiocy made me want to cry, but nothing happened. The numbness I'd carried for years became detachment, but not without feeling. The pain in my chest spread through every part of my body. I needed Sam more than I'd ever needed anything, but I'd ruined it. I'd hurt him, and worse than anything that had ever come before, I'd left him.

The bed hit the back of my legs. I sank down. The temptation to crawl under the covers and sleep a bit more was so strong, it choked me. My brain buzzed again, a discontented zap I now knew came from the drop in serotonin Meera had warned me about so many times. I stood, sat down, and stood up again. My head ached, my bones itched, and the pit of sadness in my belly made me want to die.

But there were other emotions too. Some so bizarre I knew they weren't real, and some that kept me from face planting on the bed. Pacing hurt my leg. I settled for sitting with my back to the hotel room door and listening to the world go by while I tried to figure out what the fuck the rest of my life was going to be like if I was so dependent on pills I couldn't function without them.

"You're ill," imaginary Sam reminded me. *"You need time to get better . . . as long as it takes."*

But I didn't have the capacity to believe his logic. The panicked monster in me saw only my current reality—that I was losing my mind and it was my own damn fault, and it would take more time than I could face to put that right. I choked on a sob. *I'm so fucking scared.* But there was something else. Hope, maybe? Or perhaps it was delirium, another side effect of messing my meds up. Either way, I latched onto it with both hands, crawled across the floor, and fished my phone from the tangle of sheets on the bed.

I turned it on. Sam had left me a voicemail. I hit delete without listening to it, cos if I heard his voice right now, I'd run all the way home, and yet another facet of my screwed up life would become his problem. *As if you're not his problem already. As if you haven't been his problem since the day you met.*

WhatsApp messages flashed up on the screen. I forced myself to ignore those too and searched out a contact I hadn't used for more than a year. He'd told me a hundred times to call if I needed anything. We'd never been close enough for me to believe that he'd meant it, but I didn't believe anything anymore. How could I when I couldn't trust my own mind? The beauty in it was that it left me nothing to lose.

I pressed the button and made the call.

Dom wasn't in London, and it was two days before he could get to me. He rang every few hours, trying to persuade me to let someone else into the room to help me, but I couldn't do it. I'd hurt the only soul on earth I truly trusted, and until I was well enough to fix the mess I'd left behind, there was nothing else.

He made me leave my room and meet him in the underground car park beneath the hotel. Wearing dark shades and hidden by his blacked-out windows, he looked like a roadman, but his gaze was warm when he revealed himself. He gave me a hug, a gesture that would've sent me to my knees if I hadn't already been there.

"You look wired, mate. Anything you want to tell me before I take you to my house?"

"Like what?"

"Like, are you clean? Pockets empty? I can't have that shit around my family."

Super. Even Dom thought I was a lost cause. "I haven't got any shit. I haven't been near it since last year."

His dark eyes held a suspicion I deserved, but he let it go. He put his Lexus in gear and pulled out of the car park.

It was the first time I'd seen daylight for quite some time. I winced and pulled my hood up.

Dom glanced at me. "You could do with a shower and some clean clothes."

"Yeah."

"I can take you home, if you want? Stay with you there?"

"I don't want to go home."

"Ever? Or just for today?"

I didn't have an answer that didn't end in a scream. I sank into the heated leather seat and closed my eyes. Dom put the radio on. It was the same oldies station Sam's parents listened to. I couldn't name the artists or tracks, but the familiarity hurt. I'd been so close to a normal relationship and yet so fucking removed from it at the same time. I wanted to sit in their kitchen and eat chips with them while they treated me like one of Sam's school friends. I wanted to tell them I loved their son and I'd be in their lives forever.

But I didn't know how.

Dom took me to a house in Tottenham. It was nowhere near as flashy as I expected for the amount of money I knew he still had. It was an ordinary terraced house with a cosy kitchen, a cat, and a lizard tank.

"It's a gecko," he said when he caught me looking. "I bought it by mistake when I was trying to get to know Isha's boyfriend."

"What's he like?"

"The gecko or the boyfriend?"

"Both? I think? I dunno." I shook my head to clear it. Nothing happened.

Dom pointed to an open door. "Go sit down. I'll be there in a minute."

I drifted through the door and into Dom's living room. Battered chesterfield couches took up most of the space around the kind of fireplace I'd been dreaming of for me and Sam. I sat down. Dom came into the room and crouched in front of the bundle of logs and newspaper. He lit the fire and drew a leather ottoman up to the couch. He said something. I replied. And it went on and on until the warmth of the glowing fire took me somewhere else.

"There you are." I blinked. Dom was standing in front of me in the kitchen, smiling. "I thought you'd be out for the night."

"Huh?"

"Sleeping," he clarified. "You were dead to the world. You want a shower? I stole some of Cash's clothes for you. You're about the same size."

"Cash?"

"He lives here. He's away at the moment, though, so it's just me and Lucky."

Lucky was Dom's boyfriend, the one the paps followed around and snapped at work, like they had Sam. I'd met him once, and he was as nice as he was pretty.

Not as pretty as Sam, though. Not to me.

Dom nudged me. "Shower. The clothes are in there already."

Lacking any better ideas, I followed his directions to the downstairs bathroom and got in the shower. I missed the clunky dials from the bathroom at home, but the hot water felt amazing on my sore skin. A grey puddle formed at my feet. It looked like shame. I stared at it and pondered my next move. I'd rocked up in Dom's life without a plan. He'd listened when I'd poured my heart out to him in front of the fire, but I'd passed out before he'd had time to respond.

The clothes he'd left me were hippy trousers and a T-shirt with a giant rabbit on the front.

"It's a hare, actually," he said when I slunk into the kitchen. "Cash and his dude are animal rights activists."

"Sounds fun."

"Sometimes. Listen, I'm going to make you something to eat, but I've got to tell you, I called someone while you were asleep. They're on their way over."

Panic reared in my throat, sudden and hot. "Who? Who did you call?"

"A doctor who can prescribe the drugs you need to get back on an even keel. It might take a few days to settle you, and at some point, you need to figure out why you stopped taking them in the first place, but it's a good place to start."

I fell onto a nearby stool. "I didn't do it on purpose. I forgot."

"Yeah, but why?"

I shrugged. The conversation felt off, as if I was having it with the wrong person. "I was happy. And doing different stuff, sleeping in Sam's room, doing different things in the morning. I guess I was so obsessed with him I forgot about myself."

"He didn't remind you?"

"He didn't know. I mean, he knew about the pills, but he didn't know I wasn't taking them until he found the full boxes in my drawer."

"I remember," Dom said. "You told me that he called you to let you know. Have you spoken to him since?"

"No."

"Why not? Sounds to me like he cares about you more than you deserve, and that you're crazy about him too. Why shut him out? He's got to be out of his mind with worry."

Crazy. Out of his mind. I wondered if Dom knew what those words really meant. "You're right. I don't deserve him."

"I didn't mean it literally." Dom slid a bowl of pasta across the counter and passed me a spoon. "You need to get past this block in your head when it comes to letting him love you. I get it—you don't want him exposed to the toxic bullshit people like us bring to the table, but we can't change who we are any more than him and Lucky can. Let him deal with it in his own way. If he walks away from it, at least you know it was his own decision."

"He won't walk away." It was out of my mouth before the truth of it hit me.

Dom nodded like it made perfect sense. "It would take more than a few dickheads with cameras to scare Lucky off too. Aren't you more worried he won't want to deal with the rest of it?"

"Huh?"

Dom gestured to the general state of me. "Sam sounds amazing, but if I was going to be worried about anything, it would be that a depressed ex-footballer with manic tendencies would be too much for him. It doesn't seem to worry you, so why are you so agitated about the press? They've done their worst with you already. The rest is just noise."

Sitting in Dom's kitchen, poking at his pasta while he brewed tea on a stove straight out of a Delia Smith book, logic finally found purchase in my brain. I shuddered. "I don't know why I do anything. I feel—I don't know how to explain it, like my brain and myself are disconnected, and I can't trust any of my emotions, good or bad. I don't know why the press thing freaked me out so much. It snowballed, man. I couldn't catch it."

"Understandable if you'd been off your meds for a while, and it's also totally understandable that you lost your way a bit when you and Sam got serious. Mental health and big life changes don't always mix, even if the changes are good. I had to learn that the hard way when me and Lucky first got together—I couldn't understand why he still found life so hard."

"I want to be happy."

"I know you do, mate. And I know you love Sam, or you wouldn't be here. But you know you can love him a whole lot better if you take care of yourself, right?"

I didn't. I didn't know anything. But I accepted Dom's insistence that I wait for his doctor friend before I made any more ridiculous decisions. He took my phone away to charge it while a young woman who carried her doctor kit in a SuperDry bag worked me up. She asked me a hundred questions. Poked and prodded me. Then she made me fill in a thousand forms before she handed over a three-day supply of my pills. "You'll need to go back to your regular doctor to get another prescription," she said. "If you don't go home, that is. You still have a supply there, yes?"

I nodded and swallowed the pills she'd placed in my hand. The idiot in me expected instant relief, but of course, none came. Even with the perspective Dom had gifted me, it would take days for my mood to settle.

The doctor left. Dom brought me my washed and dried clothes and hovered over me as I sat on the stairs, tying my shoes. "Are you sure you're going to be okay? You can stay here a few days if you want. Or I could drive you home?"

"It's fine." I stood, ignoring the protest from my leg. "I need to get back to normal."

"That's going to take time."

"I know, but it's not going to happen hanging around here and disrupting your life too."

"You're not disrupting my life. I understand where you are."

Of course he did. His privacy had been violated as much as mine, and he'd spent as much of his life hiding his sexuality as I had. The difference was he'd handled it like a champ, and I was a fucking mess.

A mess that needed to get back to Sam and tell him I loved him before I really did lose my mind. "I need to get home."

Dom let me go. He stood over me while I made emergency appointments to see Meera and my GP, and he called me a cab to take me back to the flat.

The journey home was something I couldn't describe. Familiar city sights blurred, and I felt like I was flying, but at the same time, dragging through tar. My heart cried out for Sam, to touch him, kiss him, breathe him in, all the while my conscience knew I had a lot of explaining to do. Sam was the best dude I'd ever known. He wouldn't drag me for my medication fuck-ups or having a legit mental health crisis, but he'd be pissed at me for running. For going dark and putting him through another level of bullshit.

I deserved his anger, and I'd take anything he threw at me.

I'd take him any way he'd have me.

The cab was on Dom's account. I scrambled out of the car and ducked inside. Upstairs, I realised I didn't have my keys, but Sam's grandfather had always left a spare hidden behind the ancient architrave.

It was still there.

I let myself in. The flat was quiet and dark; Sam wasn't home. My heart sank, but I moved through the hallway anyway in the hope that perhaps he'd dozed off on the couch.

He hadn't.

I went back to the hallway and stuck my head around his bedroom door. His drawers were hanging open and half-empty, charger cables and his laptop nowhere to be seen. With building dread, I checked his wardrobe. His overnight bag was MIA too.

He was gone.

21

Sam

Whitby wasn't the same without Micah. The precious few days we'd spent here together had erased my entire childhood, and I was adrift without him by my side.

It didn't help that my parents were shadows of their usual selves too. "Dad's all right, Mum," I said. "They said he can come home tomorrow."

My mum sighed. "Oh, I know, sweetie. I just can't help thinking about what could've happened if we hadn't been so close to the ambulance station."

I didn't want to think about it either. If there was one thing worse than worrying about Micah, it was imagining a world without my larger-than-life father filling it up. Lucky for him, medical technology was advanced enough that he could have decades more if he laid off the chips and booze.

Back at the house, I threw the chip pan away and ordered an air fryer off Amazon. Then I kissed my mum goodbye and left for the train station. I'd been gone three days. Now I knew my dad would be okay, I had to get home.

I caught a late train and sat in an empty carriage, staring out of the window. It was Sunday night, not that the day meant anything. I usually worked until it was time to go home and eat supper with Micah, but somehow we'd lost touch with our normal, and I had no fucking clue where he was. If he was okay. I'd stopped calling when I'd made the mad dash for Whitby. Then my phone service had gone down for maintenance, so I didn't know if he'd tried to call me. My phone was dead now, and the masochist in me left it that way. Not knowing seemed better than knowing, until I was stuck on a train for four hours. Then it was absolute torture. The chances of Micah calling me were slim to none, but *what if, what if, what if?*

What if he needed me?

Cynically, I had to argue that if he needed me, he'd never have left, but if I was right about his medication, then he probably had no idea what he needed. But what if I was wrong? What if he'd come off his medication under medical guidance and all that had happened was he'd realised he didn't love me after all.

Yeah. Way to make it all about you.

Selfish prick.

My maudlin thoughts kept me company all the way back to London, and I felt weighted to the grimy seat. Too tired to be awake, and yet too wired to sleep. *Micah, Micah, Micah*. I didn't know how I was going to face my empty flat. Being away had gifted me the perspective I'd needed to contemplate the possibility that Micah really might've walked away forever, but I was no closer to accepting it. How could I when I didn't truly know why he'd left?

I'd come full circle on it a dozen times and considered calling Céleste, but if she wasn't bored of my Micah angst by now, she was superhuman. I was a book that deserved a one-star DNF.

The train pulled into King's Cross. I was still the only soul in the carriage, and I stepped off in a daze. I was fifteen minutes from home, but it still seemed as if I had a lifetime to live before I got there. And it wasn't a journey I wanted to make. I didn't want to go home. The flat was barren and cruel without Micah, and after three days of angsting over my dad, I couldn't face it. *I need to get drunk.*

King's Cross was awash with shifty boozers. I found the nearest one and took a lonely pint to a quiet corner.

It didn't touch the sides. I ordered a double whisky and Coke and forced myself to sip it while I plugged my phone into a nearby socket. The phone booted up, then settled itself into a software update I'd been dodging for months.

With a heavy sigh, I picked up my drink and glanced around the bar. Was it my imagination, or were people staring at me? Not openly, of course. This was London, not Whitby where Yorkshire folk had outright asked me if I was "shagging that bender Man City player" despite the fact that it had been two years since Micah had left Manchester, and he'd been playing in London when he'd been outed.

Still, I had eyes on me nonetheless and buried myself in my phone as soon as it flashed to life, not that there was much to see. My emails were dull as mince, and I was too scared of social media to deal with Facebook for long. My usual go-to for killing time on my phone was the app for *The Guardian*. It gave me sanctuary until I came to a think piece on celebrity privacy. Sighing again, I tossed my phone on the table and downed my drink.

I got up and ordered another, leaving my phone on the table, fresh out of fucks if someone stole it or my bag with my whole life—minus Micah—stuffed inside.

No one stole anything, and the phone flashed as I returned to my table.

A message.

Micah: *i'm sorry i love u pls come home*

Micah

Wherever Sam had been, I was expecting it to take longer than fourteen minutes for him to burst through the front door.

It slammed behind him, leaving us standing in darkness, him shrouded in shadow as his shoulders heaved.

Resuming my med regime had calmed me in recent days. My mind no longer jumped from fire to the ocean and back again in ten seconds flat, but even with the chemical-induced zen, I still found it hard to believe he was really there.

I stepped forwards.

He stepped back.

"Sam—"

"What? What do you want to say, Micah?"

"I'm sorry."

"What for?"

"Everything."

"Be specific. I'm not dealing too well with my miseducated guesses."

He was so cute when he was fuming. In different circumstances, I might've found humour in his balled fists and flashing eyes, but there was nothing funny about the hurt marring his beautiful face. "I'm sorry I left. I'm sorry I made you worry. And I'm sorry I didn't take my pills. I didn't mean to. It was an accident."

"An accident?"

"Yeah. I didn't realise I'd started missing them, and then I lost my shit too much to make the connection."

It felt good to say it out loud to someone who wasn't paid to be interested. Dom had done his best, but we weren't close enough for him to care for me like a real friend. He felt sorry for me.

Sam didn't feel sorry for me. Judging by his expression, he still wanted to throttle me.

I chanced another step forwards. This time, he didn't move. My hands itched to grab his, but I kept them at my sides. I'd recovered enough to trust my feelings, but deserved or not, I couldn't handle his rejection. Not yet. "I've been to the doctor and my therapist. They said missing all those doses woulda made me really ill. And I was ill for a little while. I felt sick because of the Prozac withdrawal, like my head was a fucking spaceship, but the mood stabilisers were worse. I didn't know what I was feeling, man. I lost it . . . not as bad as before, but another few days . . . if you hadn't called . . ."

Words failed me. What if Sam hadn't called? What if he hadn't been in my room and realised my mistake? Would I ever have figured it out for myself?

Somehow I doubted it. And then what?

God, I couldn't go there. The scar on my leg throbbed in time with my thudding pulse, and the nausea I'd carried for weeks kicked up a gear.

I scrubbed a hand down my face. For days, I'd imagined this moment, how I'd crawl into the darkest corners of my mind and tell Sam anything he needed to hear to believe that it wasn't me that had run from him, that it was demons I'd relearned how to contain. But with him so close and yet so far, I didn't know where to start. Where it ended. Or how to explain the mess that had come in the middle.

"Micah."

He said my name like a prayer. I swallowed hard and met his gaze. "Yeah?"

"How long are you staying?"

"What?"

"How long are you staying? I mean, are you back? Or is this a stepping stone to something else, cos if you're moving out, I'd rather go back to the pub while you get on with it, okay? I don't need a conversation."

"I'm not moving out. Are you?"

"What?"

"Are *you*?" *Fuck it*. I stepped into his personal space. Boxed him in against the front door. "You've been gone for days too. I thought you were gone for good. That you'd maybe moved in with Céleste. I remembered that you were going to before I came here."

"That was because I couldn't afford the mortgage on my own. I work in a pub, remember? I got the place cheap from my grandad, but this is still London, and I'm not a football player."

"Do you hate me?"

Sam blinked. "Why would you ask me that?"

"Because I hurt you, and you're looking at me like I still am."

For a long moment, I feared he wouldn't answer me, that he'd turn around and walk out of the door. Or worse, open it and tell me to get the fuck out.

Then he sighed, and his shoulders flattened. His hands uncurled and he sagged forwards.

I caught him and wrapped my arms around him so tight I couldn't fathom how he was still breathing. His chest hit mine, his hips, his knees. My leg was worse right now than it had been in months, but the sensation of Sam so close soothed the tight nerves and sore muscles. I forgot about it. I forgot about everything save how it felt to have him in my arms again. "I'm sorry, Sam. I'm so fucking sorry."

He still didn't speak, but his face against my chest screamed forgiveness I didn't deserve, no matter how many times he was going to tell me that my patchy mental health wasn't my fault.

I *knew* that, as much as I knew anyone else's struggles weren't their own fault, but the sense of failure was difficult to hide from. I'd had one job—take the pills and show up to therapy—and I'd fucked it up.

"Micah."

I opened my eyes. Sam was staring at me with an expression I recognised. Relief flooded me, though I got the distinct impression he was about to tell me off. "What?"

"Stop thinking up ways to punish yourself for whatever's happened over the past few weeks, okay? None of it matters."

"It does matter."

"Do you love me?"

"Yes."

"Do you believe I love you too?"

"Yes." Of course I did. Perhaps I always had.

"Then it really doesn't matter, Micah. Not any of it. We're both here and breathing. Everything else can be fixed."

I was missing something. I tilted my head, eyebrows raised, but Sam shook his head. "Let me in the door first, yeah? I'm half cut and fucking starving."

"You smell like whisky."

"Oops." A ghost of a grin warmed his face. "Make me a sandwich then?"

As if I could refuse.

22

Sam

The sourdough bread and German ham hadn't been in the flat when I'd left. Micah had been shopping. Either that or he'd had groceries delivered, which meant he'd set up a new account or hacked into my iPad, two things way too industrious for the Micah I knew. The man who only cooked dinner if he was absolutely sure I'd eat it with him. And the bread was from the hipster bakery two streets away, a hole in the wall he must've walked to, unless someone had paid him a visit.

Curiosity—and a childish hint of jealousy—burned my throat, but I swallowed it down. I was done being a weirdo about Micah's relationships. He needed friends, and who the hell was I to get up in his business? We loved each other. I didn't own him.

Micah made me a sandwich heavy on the mustard. I needed to clear the booze from my senses. He was limping pretty bad, but the agitation that had been so rife the last time I'd seen him was gone. His eyes were still heavy, his face lined with a weariness I'd truly come to understand in the last few days, but . . . I recognised him. This was my Micah.

Yours? You don't own him, remember?

I rolled my eyes at my bitchy inner demon. Micah eyed me. "Are you having a conversation with yourself?"

"Little bit."

"Did something happen?"

"What do you mean?"

"While I was gone," he said. "You seem, uh, out of sorts, and I don't think it's all about me."

"It's not. My dad had a heart attack. That's where I've been."

"What?" Micah dropped his plate in the sink and blurred across the kitchen, instantly at my side. "When did that happen? Is he okay? Are you? What about your mum?"

His flurry of questions made my head spin. I latched onto the most important. "He's okay now. It was mild, and he had a stent fitted yesterday. My mum brought him home this morning. She's hopping mad at herself for all the fry ups she's cooked him over the years, but it is what it is. I threw the chip pan in the sea before I left."

"Seriously?"

"No. I put it in the bin, but you get the picture."

Micah sank onto the stool beside me. "I thought you'd moved out. How self-absorbed am I?"

"Not very. It's not exactly something you could've guessed, is it? I'd have told you . . . if things had been different. When you hung up on me the other day, I thought it was because you were done with me interfering in your life."

"Inter—what?" Micah frowned. "I've never thought that. And I'm glad you did this time. If you hadn't? Fuck, I don't know if I'd ever have figured it out for myself. I was losing my mind in that hotel. Dom said I was jabbering like a mad man when he picked me up."

"Dom? You mean, Dom Ramos?"

"Yeah."

"How did that happen?"

"I called him after what you said to me sank in. It took a while, and I'm sorry about that. I wasn't myself, or maybe I was, and that's the problem."

"Micah—" I shook my head. What was I doing? Shamefully, I

didn't know anywhere near enough about his mental health to tell him he was wrong. We'd lived together for months and months and months. Spent most of Christmas together. Got tipsy and sucked each other's dicks. But I had no idea why he'd been prescribed powerful psychiatric drugs beyond the fact that he'd been through a hell of a hard time.

I pushed my plate away and took his hand. "Start from the beginning."

Micah

I thought he meant the beginning of my latest crisis, but it turned out he wanted more, much more. So I told him about my first bloke-fuelled wet dream and the pubescent years I'd spent counting tiles on changing room walls to stop myself getting a boner over my naked teammates.

He laughed and it felt so fucking good. "Oh god, I feel you there. PE lessons were a nightmare, and do you know what was worse? Half the boys I was getting a sweat on over were bloody munted."

"Same. It was probably the first time in my life I thought I was going mad, cos I fancied girls too. I had no idea that I could be bi, and the thought of being gay terrified me."

"It's not so bad, you know. I do okay."

"Of course you do. But you've lived a different life. Maybe if I hadn't got into football, it would've bothered me less, but the game was the only thing I was good at, and I wanted it so much. Getting an academy place and making the first team was the dream, man."

"Came at a cost, though."

I couldn't deny it. "Yeah, but I didn't realise until I hit the big time and my life was no longer my own. When no one knew who I was, I had friends I could mess around with that had no reason to tell anyone. And later, when I'd paid them to keep quiet, there were enough girls around that I was distracted for a while."

Sam slid off his stool. He held out his hand and jerked his head towards the living room.

Silently, we traipsed into the living room. He sat where he always did, in the corner with his legs stretched out. My place had been the other end when I'd first moved in, but I'd migrated in recent months, edging closer and closer to him, even before he'd taken me to Whitby.

I sat opposite him and stretched my legs out so they touched his. "I'm sorry about your dad."

"We've done that bit. Tell me what happened when all the pretty girls went away."

"They never went away." I sent him a grin from the old days, before my face settled back into a speculative frown. "But it was too easy, and I was an arrogant prick. Hooking up with wannabe WAGs got tired, and then one day it was a hotel waiter who'd crashed the party to clear up. He told me to use a fake name on Grindr and be super low key. Said that most blokes looking for a dirty hook-up wouldn't pay too much attention to my face if I had a good bod."

"Was he right?"

"For a while. Then it started costing me money again to keep people quiet, and you know the rest."

"Not really. I know things. They don't add up to your version of events because you've never told me."

I hadn't told anyone except medical professionals. Dom wasn't a details man, and Freddie had been there. I'd never told Sam because I'd never known how. In all the conversations we'd had, never once had it occurred to me to flay myself open. Naïvely, perhaps I'd believed I didn't need to. That he knew me inside out without me having to try. But . . . I was an idiot.

My hands grew clammy. I wiped them on my sweatpants. "I guess I ran out of luck. That nearly agent I told you about managed to shut down a couple of rumours, but when him and Dom moved on, I had no fairy godfather to fix my shit. Looking back, I was unravelling for a long time, and I got sloppy, you know? Like I didn't care if I got caught. But I did care, and when it happened, I really fell apart."

"Did you—" Sam took a breath. Tried again. "Did you try and kill yourself? At the Tube station? I mean, that's what I read, but—"

"I didn't."

Something that looked suspiciously like relief crossed Sam's face. "You didn't? Because you know it wouldn't change anything, don't you? That's not why I want to know?"

I wanted to say that of course I knew that nothing I could tell him would change anything between us, but if I truly thought that, why had I never told him in the first place? It wasn't as if he hadn't given me plenty of opportunities. "I know you won't judge me or look at me differently; it's never been about that. I told you before—I think—I just can't talk about it sometimes. It was so bad back then that talking about it scares me. It puts me right back there, and I can't remember how I ever managed to leave it behind. How I didn't die on those tracks."

"Did you want to die?"

"It was an accident. I didn't jump."

Then what happened? Sam didn't verbalise the question, but he didn't have to. This was my moment to speak the truth and break the deadlock that had simmered between us since we'd met. "I fell." I twisted my hands into a convoluted tangle and forced myself to meet his gaze. "I'd done so much coke I had a fucking seizure and rolled onto the tracks. My leg got caught and burned by the current. Freddie dragged me clear, otherwise I'd have died right there on the platform. The media tried to spin it as a suicide attempt, but it really wasn't. I didn't want to die; I'd just forgotten how to live."

"Have you remembered yet?"

"Some days." I tried for a smile. Got one back in return, and the weight I'd carried for no fucking reason at all floated away. "I'm sorry. I don't know why it was so hard for me to tell you that."

"I'd imagine because it's traumatising to relive it every time someone gets nosy, and *I'm* sorry about that. I'm sorry about Freddie too. I didn't believe you when you said he was a good friend, and I should have."

"You can apologise for giving Freddie a hard time, but not for being nosy. I love that about you."

"Seriously?"

"Yeah. I've never had that with anyone before. My parents were the kind that let me get on with whatever providing I didn't bring trouble to their door. Did me a favour when I was misbehaving, but in the long run meant I never held myself to account. I regret that now."

Sam rubbed my leg in just the right place. "Do you think you'll ever reconcile with your parents?"

"Yeah. Not for a while, though. They're proud people, and I embarrassed them."

"That's awful, Micah. You were ill. It wasn't your fault."

"I know."

Silence fell over us. Sam was clearly unconvinced about my parents, but there wasn't much I could do about that. I'd spoken nothing but truth.

His body pressed against mine on the couch felt so good. I absorbed the warmth radiating from him and made it my own. Contentment settled over me. I closed my eyes. We had a long way to go, but something had shifted between us tonight and drawn us ever closer. Guilt coursed through me that I hadn't been here when he needed me, that he'd rushed home to his father alone when I should've been with him, but I couldn't fix the past, only the future. And, fuck, I loved him so much.

"Micah." Sam shook me.

I opened my eyes. For the second time that night, he stood and held out his hand. "Come on. Let's go to bed."

23

Sam

We slept in his room. Not by design; it just happened. And we really did sleep. Curled up together after a week apart, we passed out in moments, and it was well after breakfast time when I woke.

Micah was still asleep, his arm an iron weight across my middle. He was beautiful, and I had to pinch myself to check I was really awake, that he was really here and so was I.

I wondered how long he'd sleep for. The selfish git in me wanted to wake him so we could pick up where we'd left off, wading through the angst so we could finally leave some of it behind, but the rest of me reasoned that Micah needed rest. He'd been against the ropes for weeks—we both had. *Let him sleep.*

As the thought crossed my mind, he stirred, rolling onto his back and looking so serene that maybe I was dreaming after all. He sighed, his face devoid of the anxiety that had made him seem older than his years, and the temptation to touch him overwhelmed my vow to let him rest. I trailed a fingertip over his cheekbone. His eyes fluttered open and the world stopped.

Gaze bright and clear, he sat up, grinning. "You're really here."

"Says you. I thought I was dreaming."

"Yeah? What did you dream about?"

"You—"

Micah kissed me, cutting my confession dead with a sweep of his lips that sent me to cloud nine. Last night we'd gone to sleep clinging to each other like drowning men, seeking solace in the simple fact that we'd both made it home, but as he tumbled me onto my back, the current between us flowed stronger than ever, setting light to the dry tinder we'd stacked every time we'd pulled back at the last possible moment.

I wasn't wearing much—just underwear and a T-shirt. Micah stripped them from me with rough hands and chucked them aside. He was clad in his usual designer sweatpants. I pushed at the waistband, still held hostage by his fierce kiss. Chuckling, he wriggled enough for me to shove them down his thighs, taking his underwear with them. His cock hit my hand. I wrapped my fingers around his length and squeezed. God, it felt good to touch him again. To hear him gasp and moan and know his shivers were for the right reasons.

The best reasons.

Naked, we fought for dominance. Micah's leg limited his options, but he was stronger than me, heavier, taller, and perhaps he needed it more.

I found myself on my back again, caged by his arms, my legs wrapped around his waist, his dick grinding where I wanted him most, a position we'd been in before, but somehow not quite like this, cos there was no way my body had ever burned as hot as it was right now. No way I'd survive it twice.

Micah broke our kiss and pulled back. We'd neglected to turn any lights on, but I saw his every feature as if he was lit up by the fire coursing through his veins. His hair was wild, and his eyes shone bright, and perhaps for the first time since I'd known him, he was truly alive.

Or maybe it was my imagination running riot and I was seeing what I wanted to see. Micah was still unwell. A deep and meaningful conversation with added kissing hadn't changed that.

"Stop thinking."

"Hmm?"

Micah tapped my temple. "You're going off on one; I can see your brain working."

"Through my skull?"

"Yeah."

I snorted and batted his hand away. "What if I told you I was thinking about us fucking?"

"I'd say put your money where your mouth is."

His answer was quick fire, no deliberation or fretting thoughts. He held my gaze in the murky light of his room, and once again, the axis we'd built for ourselves tilted, shifting planes, and carving out a path we couldn't take back.

"Are you sure?"

He kissed me again, his dick a stone column against my abdomen. "I'm sure."

I made the mad dash to my bedroom for supplies. When I returned, Micah was sprawled on his back with his dick in his hand, waiting.

My heart jumped. *We're really doing this.* I couldn't say why it surprised me so much. Despite everything, our physical relationship had been nuclear from the start. Electric. Addictive. I tossed lube and condoms—a pack of twelve—on the bed and straddled him, sitting back against his thighs, eyeing his cock. Part of me felt like I'd never seen one before, the other quickly pictured all the ways we could do this, even with Micah's bad leg.

Micah let go of his dick and brought his hands to my hips, guiding me forwards, then back again, so he slid between my crease. I took the hint and circled my pelvis, sensation sluicing through me, heady and bright. He gasped and arched his spine. "Man, you're gonna kill me."

"Not before we come."

It was Micah's turn to snort out a laugh, but his mirth didn't last long. He let me grind down on him for a moment longer, then he moved like a snake and flipped me over.

I hit the mattress and opened my legs for him. He rolled a condom on and slicked lube over the top, balancing on his good knee. "I don't know how good I'm gonna be at this," he said.

A laugh burst free of my tight chest. "Are you serious? We've had, like, a lifetime of foreplay. I'm gonna bust in ten seconds flat."

"Yeah?"

"Yeah."

Micah loomed over me and dropped down for a kiss. Our lips met over and over and over until there were no words left. Micah rubbed lube into me, working me open with gently shaking fingers. I smiled. "You've never done that before, to anyone."

He shrugged. "I never cared enough. And there's a lot of things I've never done. You know you're the first boy I ever kissed?"

"Yeah, you said." The privilege of it added to the glow blooming in my stomach. God knew how many dudes Micah had picked up on Grindr over the years, but as he aligned our bodies and eased inside me, I knew with absolute certainty that he'd never gazed at anyone the way he gazed at me then. As if he was drinking me in, forever mapping every facet of me.

Micah had a big dick, and I hadn't been with anyone since last spring—a misguided hook-up of my own; a clumsy fumble that had underscored the crush I had on my new roommate. My body stretched and burned, but I welcomed the discomfort and let the pain add to the thrill of Micah sliding inside me.

Pain turned to pleasure. I tightened my legs around Micah and held him still.

"Am I hurting you?" he whispered.

I grinned. "Nah. I like it."

"Always knew you were a dirty bastard."

"Can't deny it."

"Uh-huh." Micah thrust his hips, his aim perfect considering he was holding this shit down with one leg. "Tell me what you want then. You like it hard?"

"I like it all."

"All?"

"Yeah."

Still moving inside me, building up to a killer rhythm, his sex-hazed stare grew thoughtful, but it was gone before I could question it, erased by the inferno he was stoking with his cock.

The time for talk was over. Micah fucked me until his leg gave out, then I rolled him over and rode him, staring down at him, transfixed by his every ragged breath, his flushed skin, and the possessive glint in his eyes. I was on top, but there was no doubt he was owning me. He gripped my hip with one hand and slammed the other down on my shoulder, controlling the pace as he thrust up into me. My cock bounced between us, so hard it hurt. I gripped it and squeezed, and combined with the sensation of Micah surging inside me, I was done.

Orgasm ambushed me. "Fuck, I'm gonna come."

Micah groaned and drove into me like a piston. He swelled inside me and pulled my head down so his lips reached my ear. "Do it. Come with me."

I didn't need telling twice. My self-control and stamina was at an all-time low, and as Micah fell apart beneath me, white noise filled my head, and I came harder than I could ever remember.

Micah came with a gravelly moan, clutching me to him, his fingers tangled in my hair. He was breathing so hard I thought something was wrong. Then he pulled back and smiled at me, and I knew that even with whatever giant bumps in the road we came across, everything was going to be okay.

Aftershocks rattled through me. I wanted him inside me forever, but Micah didn't have a bionic dick. He slipped out of me. I sighed at the loss, but his arms around me softened the blow.

His mouth on my neck, my jaw, my lips was even better. He kissed me like the very first time and rolled me reverently onto my back. "I love you."

I stroked my thumb over his cheekbone. "I love you, too."

Micah fell asleep again.

Hungry, I forced myself away from him and into the kitchen. There was still bread and ham. Eggs and a handful of vegetables. I made a giant omelette and stuck it under the grill to finish off. Then I made thick slices of toast with butter and pretended my dad didn't have to spend the rest of his life on statins and eating Benecol.

I was texting my mum when Micah limped into the kitchen. "You should've woken me. I'm not supposed to sleep too much during the day."

"Why?"

He shrugged. "Bad habits."

I waited a moment to see if he'd elaborate. He didn't, but he did move close enough that I could feel his body heat and smell his familiar scent. He peered over my shoulder at the message I was sending my mum. "She okay?"

"Yeah. Just facing the music. She told me to hug you from her while I was up there."

"Go on then."

I put my phone down and wrapped my arms around him. He was bed-warm and solid, and his answering embrace was glorious. I didn't want it to end, but my grumbling stomach forced me to let him go. "Are you hungry?"

Micah nodded absently and sat on a stool. "Did you tell your mum I was MIA?"

"Nope."

"Why not?"

"Two reasons." I flipped the omelette onto the board and sliced it up. "Firstly, that she had enough to worry about, and second, I needed a break from it. If I'd told her, she'd have wanted to talk it to death, even with all the drama going on with my dad, and I couldn't face it."

"I'm sorry."

"What for?"

"For putting you in a position where my shit alienated you from your family. It's wrong, man."

"You didn't alienate me from anything. I made a conscious decision not to tell her."

Micah chewed on his bottom lip. I freed it with my thumb and dragged him in for a quick kiss. "Look, can we not do the blame thing? I feel like we're stuck in a misunderstood plot hole as it is."

"A what?"

"The big misunderstanding. It's an overused plot device in fiction, in my opinion, at least. My lit teacher loves it. Says it's representative of a modern world that's forgotten how to communicate without technology."

"The fuck are you talking about?"

"Never mind." I loaded plates and brought them to the counter. We ate in silence for a few minutes before a question that had been burning me up inside abruptly couldn't wait any longer. "Can I ask you something?"

"If you want."

"It's kind of personal."

"So?"

"So, I want to give you the chance to tell me to mind my own business."

"Why?"

"Why not?"

Micah shook his head. "So I can fuck you till you bite a hole in my pillow, but you can't ask me a simple question? That's not how it works."

I rolled my eyes. "It's not about sex."

"It doesn't have to be. Ask me anything. I don't care."

His candour was so refreshing I glanced at the window to see if it was open. It wasn't, obviously. And when I looked back at Micah, his expression was more open than I'd ever seen. I took a breath and blurted out words I'd been so sure would push him away. "What are the mood stabilisers in your drawer for? I googled them, but all I got back was bipolar, and I'm kind of hoping that's not a diagnosis you were afraid to tell me about."

"I'm not bipolar." Micah finished his breakfast and pushed his plate away. "They assessed me for it when I was in hospital but decided I had PTSD with manic tendencies. And depression. I didn't have the right mood pattern for bipolar disorder or a bunch of other stuff."

"Wow. That's still a pretty hefty diagnosis. Did it scare you?"

"Nah. They're just words. And I didn't take them in at the time."

"Can I ask you something else?"

"Of course."

"Would you have played again? If you hadn't hurt your leg? After you got outed, I mean."

The flicker I'd been waiting for finally clouded Micah's gaze. He sucked in a deep breath and slowly let it out. "I honestly don't know. There aren't any openly queer players in the top leagues, you know that. And I wasn't good enough for any club to want me to be their wokety-woke poster boy. Even without the dick scandals, I was a pain in the arse."

I shifted gingerly. "Class clown?"

"Something like that." Micah sighed again and reached for my hand. "I wish it had been as simple as just football and liking a bit of cock; maybe I could've styled it out. But the truth is, I'd been ill for a long time before I fell on those train tracks, and compared to putting myself back together, kicking a ball around a field doesn't mean much to me anymore."

"Doesn't it?"

"No. I like hanging out with Mr Chan down the gym and watching him do incredible things with old bones and aching joints. I like showing Mrs Patterson that if she can get in and out of the pool by herself, she can get on the bus. It means something, and I'm happy with that. And you know what?"

"What?"

Micah drew me in for a kiss. "I'm happy with *you*. Now can we fuck again or what?"

24

Micah

"I'm happy with you."

But as ever, it wasn't that clear cut. We had sex every day for a week. It was amazing, but I still felt like I'd fallen halfway down treasure mountain and left my bag at the top. There was more to come. So much more. Being inside Sam, loving him in every way possible, blew my recovering mind, but I needed something else.

And he knew it, obviously, cos he was fucking psychic or some shit. He packed me off for a therapy appointment and told me not to come back until I'd unpicked whatever was bothering me. In months gone by, I might have scoffed and told him it was nothing, but I was working too hard on myself right now to let a weevil in my brain fuck me up. *And*, I'd meant it when I'd told Sam I was happy with him. Sadness and despair had been my companions for long enough that I knew the difference.

"I'm glad you've made progress in your relationship with Sam," Meera said. "You've often spoken of him in a way that let me know how important he is to you."

I picked a loose thread on the arm of her couch. "Have I?"

"Yes, and remember that we were working together before you met him, so I've seen first-hand the difference his friendship has made to your recovery."

"You think I'm dependent on him?"

"Not at all. Would you like to explore why you chose to see something negative in what I've said?"

I rolled my eyes, and she smiled. We had spent long months unravelling my unhealthy thought patterns. These days, I made them up to needle her, not that it worked. She was too sharp for me. "I love him," I said. "Is that positive enough for you?"

"It'll do. But I'm getting the feeling you're agitated about something revolving around that. Do you know what it is?"

"Nope. It's got something to do with sex, though."

"You're having a sexual relationship?"

I nodded and heat flooded my cheeks, though I couldn't say why. Meera knew I'd wet myself when I'd fallen onto the train tracks. Had visited me in the hospital when I'd been in restraints. And we'd talked about sex before—the girls, the boys, escorts, and Grindr. But Sam was different. Precious. I didn't want to dissect what we had with anyone but him.

This isn't about him, though. It's you. It's always been you. "I think I . . . um. I think I want to do something with him I've never done before—well, not that I can remember, anyway."

Silence. I could almost see the cogs in Meera's brain turning as she deciphered my vague statement. "Okay," she said slowly. "I'm not going to ask you to spell it out for me—I don't think the details matter—but do you think you could try and tell me why it's something you need to talk to me about instead of Sam?"

"How do you know I haven't talked to Sam about it?"

"Educated guess."

Damn her and whatever the certificates on her wall meant. "I've talked to him about it in my head, but every time I try to do it for real, I feel stupid."

"Why?"

"Because he's, like, a fucking god, and I'm this idiot who's spent his whole adult life believing that getting my dick wet was real sex."

I finished on a half shout that made me feel even worse, but every word of my rant was true. Sam never faltered. His hands and tongue were sure of their path, and every touch and caress was fucking perfect. I craved that perfection in places I hadn't known existed before him, dark parts of my soul that only he could bring to life. Damn it, I *needed* him to fuck me.

A lightbulb lit up my brain. Meera raised an eyebrow and said more words, but I barely heard her. Jesus. *That* was it? Had I been watching him fall apart around my dick this whole time consumed by jealousy cos I wanted it too?

It can't be that simple.

But there was that word again: simple. Anxious minds were complicated places to be. Had I lost a primal urge to black thoughts and overthinking?

Figuring out the answer to that would take time I didn't want to waste. I played Meera's game for ten more minutes, then bid her a hasty goodbye. As I turned to leave, she caught my hand. "You've done well today, Micah. Think on this before our next session: you've spent a lifetime unable to say what you want and be proud of it. Perhaps it's time to change that."

Sam wasn't home when I burst through the front door. The born-again virgin in me was relieved. The rest of me was so antsy I had to take a cold shower to calm the fuck down.

My leg didn't appreciate the shock. My muscles seized, and I spent the next half hour apologising with heat and lavender oil. I smelt like an old people's home by the time Sam came back.

He had a pizza box in one hand, a bag from the bakery in the other. "I take it you didn't have any lunch?"

I didn't know what I wanted more, the garlicky concoction in the box, the custard tarts I could see through the white paper bag, or him looming over me, his hard dick easing me open.

A heatwave rolled through me.

Sam tilted his head sideways. "Are you okay?"

I nodded slowly. "Yeah. Just, uh, hot from the shower."

"And the heat pack?"

"Yeah."

He didn't look convinced, but that was a face I was used to after the last few months. And for once, I had the answer to put it right. I just had to find the words.

Sam disappeared into the kitchen. I shoved the heat pack aside and limped after him.

He opened the pizza box. Prawn-garlic pizza appeared like magic, but the growl in my stomach had nothing on the roar in my heart. I had to be as close to him as possible.

I rounded the counter and pushed my way into his personal space. He dropped the bakery bag and gripped my wrist, tugging me to where I needed to be. "Hey there," he whispered. "Something you want?"

"Yeah, but not what you think."

He frowned, and the pressure of him crammed against me faded a touch. *Fuck that.*

I crowded him some more. "I need to say something, but I feel like a Class A twat saying it, so don't laugh, okay?"

"I never laugh at you."

"Not true. You laughed at me this morning."

"You called the washing machine a motherfucking douchebag."

"It is a douchebag. It's been stuck on the cold cycle for days—fuck, that's not the point. Just let me talk, okay? Or I'll never say it, and I'll carry on being as annoying as I've been for the last few days."

"You're not annoying."

"Liar."

Sam started to smile but caught himself and pursed his lips, trepidation creeping into his wide gaze. "I'm listening."

"I want you to fuck me."

His eyebrows shot up as if I'd stuck a Taser between his ribs. "What?"

"I want you to fuck me." Repeating it was as surreal as saying it the first time. "Like, really fuck me, on top, you know? I've never wanted to do it again since the first time, but I want it so much with you, I can't think about anything else."

"I—" Sam shook his head slightly. Banged it on my shoulder. "Wow. Damn. I'm sorry, it's just. Fuck. That was the last thing on earth I expected you to say. I thought you were about to drop something awful on me."

Of course he did. And I couldn't blame him for that, but I was too hot for him to get bogged down in self-loathing. That shit could wait, perhaps long enough for it to go away on its own. Right now, I had room in my soul only for Sam.

I found his hands and squeezed them. "Sorry if I've blindsided you with this. We don't have to, like, actually do it. I just needed you to know before I set myself on fire with it."

"Interesting image." Sam kissed my knuckles. "How long have you felt like this?"

"I don't know."

"You don't know?"

"It didn't come together until I was with Meera this afternoon. Before then it was just a feeling I couldn't describe."

His gaze grew heated enough to quicken my pulse. "Can you describe it now?"

"Uh." I licked my lips. "Can I show you instead?"

In answer, Sam pushed off the counter and shouldered past me, gesturing for me to follow. He led us to the bedroom and spun to face me. "Micah, you can show me anything you want, and when you're done, do you know what I'm going to do?"

I swallowed thickly and shook my head.

Sam stepped closer, his lips inches from mine. "I'm gonna fuck you till you beg me to stop."

Sam

Dirty talk still freaked Micah out, but I couldn't help the filth on my tongue. I'd always been a horny bastard, but the chemistry between us was something else. He wanted me to fuck him, and only an apocalypse was going to stop me.

Or Micah. Whatever happened, I was still listening. Always.

I ran my hands up his bare arms. I needed him naked, but despite a desire for him so deep my eyeballs were pulsing in time with my heart, I knew we couldn't rush this. That one wrong move could scare him off. Reason told me that other days would come, but there was nothing reasonable about the way my body ached for Micah, so I moved slowly, with gentle hands, and undressed him with the reverence he deserved.

When he was bare to me, he lay back on the bed, sharp eyes tracking my every move—and the condoms and lube I retrieved from the bedside drawer. I put them within easy reach and focussed on him. The curtains were drawn, casting shadows over his glorious body. I kissed my way from his lips, to his chest, to his belly, and his dick, then I took him in my mouth and swallowed him down, revelling in his startled gasp. His legs fell open and his hips canted.

He buried his hands in my hair. "Fuck, *Sam*."

My name on his lips kicked my pulse up a gear. For long minutes, I ground his cock against the back of my throat, recalling every second I'd had him inside me. Every thrust and drive. Every wave of mind-blowing pleasure. It was a ride like nothing else, perhaps the only precious minutes I'd ever truly been free of all else. I wanted that for him. I wanted him to feel nothing but how beautiful he was and how much I fucking loved him.

Slowly, I reached for the lube, still working him with my mouth. In my head we had a sensible conversation about how far he'd gone with this before, but my heart didn't want to know if anyone else had ever slid careful, slick fingers inside him. This moment was mine. It was *ours*.

I released Micah's dick from my mouth, gripped his good leg, and eased it aside. He rose up on his elbows, watching. The apprehension in his gaze was hard to miss. I tried for a smile. He bit his lip and sucked in a shaky breath. "Do it," he whispered. "I trust you."

Did he? If you'd asked me a week ago, I might've said no, but Micah was changing with every day that he learned to trust himself, and this time, I believed him.

I worked him open, keeping his cock in my mouth to ground him. Tension warred with pleasure, and pleasure won. Sweat dampened Micah's skin. He moaned low and sweet, and his thighs quivered. I found his prostate and grazed it.

He arched from the bed. "Fuckin' Christ, do that with your dick."

"Are you sure?"

"*Sam*."

Despite the vow I'd made when I'd led him in here, I was never going to make him beg for anything. I sat back on my heels and rolled a condom onto my aching dick. He was watching me again, lip caught between his teeth. This time I left it there and considered my options. Micah had pretty much bent me in half and fucked my brains out, but his leg didn't flex like mine anymore, and the last thing I wanted was to cause him more pain.

I rolled him onto his side and pressed up behind him, one hand gripping the back of his neck, the other his hip. "This okay?"

"Yes. I want this. I want *you*."

I pushed inside him, breaching the instant resistance his body threw up, inch by slow inch.

Wet heat enveloped me. *Shit*, he was so tight. I'd never felt anything like it. Pleasure shocks zipped through me, and I dug my fingers into his flesh, pressing my head between his shoulder blades. *I can't do this. I can't be careful with him. I want him too damn much.*

Micah reached back. He didn't say anything. Just found my wrist and wrapped his fingers around it.

I closed my eyes, breathing as deeply as my taut nerves allowed. My cock slid inside him another inch, then another and another until I could go no further, and I swear stars exploded, the ones behind my eyes, at least. "So fucking good."

Micah hummed, his fingers still a vice around my wrist. He circled his hips a fraction. More crazy sensations rocked me, and I forced myself to be present and not lose myself to this moment. I drew back, dragging my cock with me, watching with bated breath as Micah instinctively chased me. "Yeah. Come and get it."

If it hurt, he didn't let me know. He ground back on me, finding a groove that suited him until I was losing my fucking mind. Patience and coherent thought abandoned me. I tightened the hand still gripping his neck and thrust into him.

Micah cried out and scrabbled for balance on the bed. I did it again, and again, and again, daring him to stop me.

He didn't, so I kept fucking him, driving inside him over and over as filth poured out of my mouth and into his ear. Flesh slapped against flesh. Tender moments became heady pleasure as Micah flexed and arched against me, my name a chant on his lips.

He fell onto all fours, his chest flush with the mattress, hips in the air. Knowing he couldn't hold the position for long, I hunched over him and screwed him harder.

"Oh fuck, oh fuck." Micah widened his stance. "I'm gonna come so fucking hard."

Yeah, you are. I leaned back, changing the angle. A ragged groan tore from my chest, and Micah answered me with a strangled yell. *That's it, that's it.* And then it hit me that I needed him to come because my own release was bearing down on me like a fucking avalanche, picking up speed and might with every drive inside him. "Do it. Come."

As if he needed my permission. Watching him fall apart was everything. He clenched tight around me and went rigid with pleasure, his low moans rising in pitch until he was hoarse and gasping for breath.

He fell slack in my arms as it faded, but I wasn't done with him. I surged inside him, chasing my own release, and just when I thought I'd combust, the force of it knocked me sideways. Wet warmth pulsed where we were joined, and I came with a crazed shout that rattled the walls.

It took a moment for the dust to settle and for me to come back to myself. I fought for breath, shaking in every limb, and piece by piece, the real world returned.

Micah was wrecked. I slipped out of him and tossed the condom. Then I eased him onto his back and smoothed his hair out of his face. "All right?"

He hummed, eyes shut, a soft half-smile playing on his lips. "Ask me in a minute."

It was going to take longer than that, but I let it go and lay down beside him, the lingering heat of orgasm enough to keep us both warm. For a while, he was so quiet, I wondered if he'd fallen asleep. Then he sighed. "I feel like you've slipped me a magic pill."

I glanced at him and found him wide awake and staring. "A good magic pill?"

"Yeah. I've never felt more myself than I do right now."

I sat up and flicked the lamp on. Soft light surrounded us like the hug of an old friend. "I wish it was that simple, for lots of reasons. But you know I'd never change anything about you, don't you?"

"I think so." Micah sat up on his elbows. Soft smudges still coloured the skin beneath his eyes and I wondered if they'd ever fade, but beneath it all, something else simmered—hope, perhaps—that I'd never seen in him before. "And you know what? I'm okay with myself too. I'm gonna be on these meds for a long time, but I'd take them forever if I needed to and not care. I'm . . . happy, because I want to be. Does that make sense?"

"Not much about anything makes sense, Micah."

He cupped my face in his heated palm and gifted me a perfect smile. "This does."

25

Sam

Two months later

Exams sucked, especially when you were years older than every fucker in the room. But I'd take one every day if it meant walking out to find Micah waiting for me on the steps with our packed bags and train tickets.

"Come on." He took my hand, not giving a single shit who was looking. "Let's go."

We caught the train north. I dozed against Micah's shoulder while he flicked through the training programmes he'd written for my dad. He'd been obsessing over them for weeks, researching heart health at the library while I'd revised for my exams, and drawing up meal plans and activity logs until he had a tidy folder of tools to keep my dad away from the friendly cardiologist. So far, he was refusing to let my dad pay him, but I was working on that.

Five hours later, we trudged into my parents' house. My dad was playing darts at the pub and drinking lime and soda. Micah stepped out to check up on him while I unpacked for our week-long stay and caught up with my mum.

"He looks different every time I see him," she remarked from the doorway of the bedroom.

I glanced over my shoulder. "He got a haircut yesterday."

"That's not what I meant."

"I know." And I really did. Micah worked on his recovery every single day, and the change in him was undeniable. He was a man no longer existing, but living. And loving. Barely an hour passed without him reminding me of that—a call, a message, a heated stare, or a sweet note left on the fridge. Sometimes it felt like I'd been dropped into the world I'd dreamt up when I was a horny teenager waiting for my first kiss, and that it was only a matter of time before reality kicked me in the nuts, then warm arms would slide around me from behind, he'd kiss my neck, and I'd remember that nothing I'd ever imagined came close to the real thing.

Micah was the man of anyone's dreams.

Later that night, we ate chicken salad and brown rice with my parents before sloping off to bed.

"Use protection," my dad called.

I cringed, glad I couldn't see Micah's face. Under the glare of the occasional pap, he was still getting used to bringing us into the outside world, and sex jokes with my dad? Yeah. He wasn't there yet.

Or so I thought.

Assumed.

Whatever. *I* was getting better at not doing that.

Upstairs, he pushed me against the closed bedroom door. "You brought some, right?"

"Some what?"

"Duh. Protection."

"Are you asking me if I brought condoms and lube to my mum's house?"

"Yes."

I held his gaze for a moment, then shrugged. "Of course I did. In the wash bag."

I didn't add that we probably didn't need them anymore, given that neither one of us was banging anyone else. Or that there were probably plenty still stashed around my room from said horny teenage years that I'd forgotten about. Micah didn't need to know how prepared fourteen-year-old me had been for something that hadn't happened until three years later. Strawberry-flavoured Durex anyone? Ribbed for no one's pleasure?

"What are you laughing at?"

I blinked. Micah was in front of me with a condom that was less like a wellington boot and a bottle of our favourite lube. Somehow I'd missed him crossing the room and back again. "Nothing. I'm just trying to figure out how we're going to do this without my dad banging on the ceiling and telling us to keep it down."

"You'll have to be quiet."

"Me?"

"Yeah. I'm gonna fuck you, cos I don't trust myself not to let the neighbours know if we do it the other way round."

"I like making you scream."

"I know, but not here, though, mate. I have to face your mother in the morning."

I took pity on him and stripped my clothes in record time. Fucking Micah was a privilege I never took for granted, but I couldn't deny that having him own me, inside and out, was just as good. Sometimes it was hard to choose what I wanted more, so perhaps my parent's dozing off in front of the ten o'clock news was doing me a favour.

Micah laid me down on the bed and pressed his hand over my mouth. He fucked me long and slow, easing whimpers and shudders with every teasing stroke of his dick inside me.

When we'd first started fucking, he'd often found my prostate by chance. Now he was like a goddamn laser, and my only solace in the glorious torture was the knowledge that I'd get my own back the second we got home.

We came together, muffling groans with a kiss that went on and on. I was dimly aware of Micah leaving the bed and returning, and as ever, the simple joy of sharing a bed made my heart ache in the very best way. After weeks of exam stress, I was dog tired but found myself awestruck and gazing at him. I didn't want to miss a moment. I'd fail every exam I ever took if I could just have this.

Next thing I knew, though, it was morning, and I was alone. Even Micah's clothes were gone, which made sense, unless I wanted him padding around my ma's house naked like he did at home.

A wave of longing washed over me. I loved my parents to death, but *fuck*, there was nothing quite like locking the doors, pulling the blinds, and pretending we were the only souls on earth.

Voices sounded beneath me, coming from the kitchen. Grumbling, I got dressed and stomped downstairs. Micah was at the kitchen table helping my mum go through her new pile of charity shop recipe books while my dad chopped a gigantic pineapple at the counter. A year ago, the scene would've been so bizarre I could only have dreamt it, and it dawned on me that we didn't need to be the only souls on earth to be all that we were to each other. Right here, right now was everything I'd ever need.

Micah

Four months later

Sam aced his exams. I knew he would, but until he opened that envelope, he'd had no idea. "You really thought you'd failed?"

He shrugged and muttered something I didn't catch over the racket in the Noble Fox. Ignoring the urge to check myself in a public place, I crowded him into the dimly lit corner we'd chosen to celebrate his results and forced him to look at me. "Why would you think that? You worked like a demon for those papers."

"Yeah, but . . ."

"But what?"

"I took a month off when you were ill. I didn't mean to. I was just, I don't know, so consumed by other things, I never got round to doing any real work. I'm amazed I was graded at all, let alone that it was an A."

And there it was: if he'd failed, it would've been my fault. At least, that's where my brain wanted to take me, but I was wise to that shit by now. A guilt trip didn't do either of us any favours. Besides, I'd have burned the world down to be with Sam if he'd needed me as much as I'd needed him back then, and I knew he loved me just as hard.

I brushed a quick kiss on his exposed throat and scooted back to my seat.

He watched me, amused, and winked at someone over my shoulder. Céleste, no doubt. The two of them got a real kick out of me smooching on Sam in public. Me? I was learning to ignore the eyes on me and get on with my life. If I wanted to kiss my boy in Sainsbury's, I was gonna do it no matter how many clowns put it on Instagram.

Some days it really was that easy. Others, I still had panic attacks when Sam's face popped up in the tabloids and his mum rang to check he was okay. The guilt was vicious. Without me, Sam could do anything he wanted, any time, any place. With me, there was always the risk the whole world would see before he was ready.

Before *we* were ready.

Sam leaned impossibly closer and tapped my temple. "Thinking already? It's barely lunchtime."

"I'm a morning person, remember?"

"I do. I also remember that look on your face. What are you fretting about?"

"I'm not fretting."

"Liar. Is it the dude in the corner hiding his hands behind the Waitrose bag? Cos I think he's having a wank, not taking pictures."

"Nice." This time I had zero urge to look over my shoulder. "But I'm still not fretting. I was just thinking how chill I feel today, compared with last Tuesday when I wanted to deck that pap loitering outside the gym."

"You only wanted to deck him because I was there. You'd have ignored him if you'd been on your own."

"But I wasn't on my own, was I? And I don't like being on my own."

"That's sweet. And it's even sweeter that you turn into an angry bear every time some tool points a camera at me, but you should save your energy, boo. I really don't care."

My scowl deepened. "Why do you keep saying you don't care?"

"Because it's true. It's not like I get caught with my pants down, is it? Sometimes they take pictures of us and I see things I might not have noticed if they hadn't. It's like the intrusion gifts me a perspective I need, you know?"

"Nope. You're talking shit."

Sam laughed, and the sound washed most of my worries away. We'd had this conversation a thousand times over the last few months, and often I really did find it hard to believe he was so blasé about the limits on our privacy, but other times it made sense. Sam had made a conscious decision not to let my reality affect his present, and I was more in awe of him for that than almost anything else.

Almost. Cos he was still the cleverest motherfucker I'd ever known.

I was about to kiss him again when a new face dropped into the seat beside me.

Freddie.

Damn. It had been a minute. Out of habit, I cast a wary glance at Sam, but he wasn't where I'd left him. He was reaching across the table to give Freddie a hug and kiss on the cheek, a sight that surprised me now as much as it had done when he'd first done it a few months ago. They liked each other these days, you see. It was *me* who had trouble being my full bisexual self around Freddie when I'd spent so many years not. It didn't seem to matter that he'd seen me at my absolute lowest; showing him my happy was . . . weird. For me, anyway. He didn't give a remote fuck. He embraced Sam like a brother he showed a little too much affection for and kissed him right back.

Prick.

I drank my Diet Coke and watched them interact for a while. It should've warmed my pinched little heart that they got on so well, but I'd learned something about myself since I'd escaped the fog of mental illness enough to have an actual adult relationship—I was possessive as fuck, and even my heterosexual BFF making eyes at my dude wound me up.

Wound Sam up too . . . in that it made him inexplicably want to jump me.

"So . . . I have news," Freddie said when he was done rattling my cage. "You'll see it online in the morning, but I wanted you to be the first to know that I'm transferring back up north."

"To Manchester?"

He shook his head. "Nope. Merseyside. Gonna play for the Blues while I get some other shit sorted out."

"Other shit?"

Freddie swigged his drink, then set his glass down with a sigh. "Turns out watching you go through everything you did triggered something in me I need to unpick. This life is hard, man. I don't want it to swallow me whole."

It made sense, and there were many footballers who needed as much therapy as I'd had. More. But in all the years I'd known Freddie, I'd never once thought him one of them. He made everything look so easy.

Sam kicked me under the table. I was staring. "Fuck." I reached for Freddie and finally embraced him the way I should've when he'd arrived. "I'm sorry, mate. Can I do anything to help?"

"Nah. Not unless you wanna *help* me through the dry spell I forced on myself when I needed some time to think. So long without a woman is making me realise how pretty you are."

I rolled my eyes.

Sam smirked and shook his head at Freddie. "You couldn't handle him."

Freddie laughed. "Nah, probably not. But I can handle you, sweetheart."

"Go on then."

"All right, all right," I broke in before Freddie figured out the hard way that he wasn't cut for a game of gay chicken, but it was too late. A dude in a hoodie broke into our space with a phone camera and snapped us with Sam's hand on Freddie's thigh and my arms halfway around both of them. The headline flashed into my mind as the pap melted into the crowd: "*Crazy Gay Micah Continues His Quest to Corrupt Freddie Santos.*" It was so ridiculous and yet so plausible, even I had to laugh. And I had to let it go. What did I care if the whole world thought I was having a threesome with my lover and a fuck-hot footballer?

Yeah, that's right. I couldn't deny Freddie was hot.

"You so would," Sam teased me on the way home.

"Would not." I flicked a sesame seed from my burger bun at him. "And even if I wanted to, he's straight, remember? And an active footballer. We all know how that turns out."

Sam stole a handful of my chips, despite having a giant container of his own, and shot me a mischievous look. "He *appears* straight, and he won't be a footballer forever, baby."

He was joking. I was almost sure of it. But the details didn't matter as we meandered our way home. Sam leaned against me while he stole my food, and I couldn't think of a time when talking about dude sex had ever been so easy, so free, and so wholesomely fun. Could I share Sam with my friend? With *anyone*? Probably not, but laughing about it made me feel like a fucking king.

I was in love with my roommate, my best friend, and my soulmate all wrapped up in a perfect bundle of long limbs and soft hair, and I wouldn't change a thing.

FURTHER READING

Curious about Dom? His story can be found in LUCKY, in which you'll also catch a glimpse of Micah in his footballer days.

NEWSLETTER

Get a free story!

For the most up to date news and free books, subscribe to my newsletter HERE.

This is a zero spam zone. Maximum number of emails you will receive is one per month.

PATREON

Not ready to let go of Micah and Sam? Or looking for sneak peeks at future books in the series? Alternative POVs, outtakes, and missing moments from **all** Garrett's books can be found on her Patreon site. Misfits, Slide, Strays...the works. Because you know what? Garrett wasn't ready to let her boys go either.

Pledges start from as little as $2, and all content is available at the lowest tier.

ABOUT GARRETT LEIGH

Bonus Material available for all books on Garrett's Patreon account. Includes short stories from Misfits, Slide, Strays, What Remains, Dream, and much more. Sign up here: https://www.patreon.com/garrettleigh

Facebook Fan Group, Garrett's Den... https://www.facebook.com/groups/garre...

Garrett Leigh is an award-winning British writer, cover artist, and book designer. Her debut novel, Slide, won Best Bisexual Debut at the 2014 Rainbow Book Awards, and her polyamorous novel, Misfits was a finalist in the 2016 LAMBDA awards, and was again a finalist in 2017 with Rented Heart.

In 2017, she won the EPIC award in contemporary romance with her military novel, Between Ghosts, and the contemporary romance category in the Bisexual Book Awards with her novel What Remains.

When not writing, Garrett can generally be found procrastinating on Twitter, cooking up a storm, or sitting on her behind doing as little as possible, all the while shouting at her menagerie of children and animals and attempting to tame her unruly and wonderful FOX.

Garrett is also an award winning cover artist, taking the silver medal at the Benjamin Franklin Book Awards in 2016. She designs for various publishing houses and independent authors at blackjazzdesign.com, and co-owns the specialist stock site moonstockphotography.com

Connect with Garrett
www.garrettleigh.com

ALSO BY GARRETT LEIGH

Kiss Me Again

Lucky

Cash

Jude

Slide

Rare

Circle

Misfits

Strays

Dream

Whisper

Believe

Crossroads

Bullet

Bones

Bold

House of Cards

Junkyard Heart

Rented Heart

Soul to Keep

My Mate Jack

Lucky Man

Finding Home

Only Love

Heart

What Remains

What Matters

Between Ghosts

www.ingramcontent.com/pod-product-compliance
Lightning Source LLC
Chambersburg PA
CBHW020611310726
48979CB00008B/1431/J
* 9 7 8 1 9 1 3 2 2 0 2 7 3 *